ART OF THE KILL

PRAISE FOR WES RAND

"The unconventional collected works of Wes Rand was recommended to me. I can say these are not for the whimsical as you'll wish that only bandits, outlaws, and wildlife, are the only things to fear. Bring a gun as you sit down to read and pray you are not on the wrong side of Major Neville Stryker."

— **DIANE KAWASAKI**, WRITER AND STAR OF TLC'S HIT SHOW MY LITTLE LIFE

"Gritty, dark, and fast-paced—If you love frontier action, Wes Rand's EVIL STRYKER SERIES will knock you out of the saddle."

— *ERIC J. GUIGNARD*, AWARD-WINNING AUTHOR, AND EDITOR, INCLUDING *AFTER DEATH...* AND *BAGGAGE OF ETERNAL NIGHT*, BRAM STOKER AWARD-WINNER

"As a filmmaker, I can see the vibrant images come to life on every page as Evil Stryker crosses every line of decency and yet leaves the women wanting him and the men wanting to be him. Wes has created an anti-hero of devastating impact."

— **VINCENT ROCCA**, WRITER/DIRECTOR OF *KISSES AND CAROMS*, AUTHOR OF *11 SIMPLE STEPS TO TURN A SCREENPLAY INTO A MARKETABLE MOVIE: OR, HOW I GOT A $10K MOVIE TO GROSS $1 MILLION THROUGH WARNER BROS*

"A wild ride through the old west, filled with unforgettable characters and plenty of action. This series hits all the marks! You're going to love Evil Stryker!"

— **JOHN PALISANO,** VICE PRESIDENT OF THE
HORROR WRITERS ASSOCIATION AND BRAM
STOKER AWARD-WINNING AUTHOR OF *NIGHT OF
1,000 BEASTS*

"Evil Stryker operates like a confident, skilled executioner across its violent Western landscape."

— **DALLAS SONNIER**, PRODUCER OF BONE
TOMAHAWK

ALSO BY WES RAND

Left to Die - Book 1

Cross Cut - Book 2

Payback is Hell - Book 3

To Die For - Book 4

The Christmas Slay - Book 5

Trouble in Tahoe - Book 6

ART OF THE KILL

Book VII in the Evil Stryker Series

WES RAND

ART OF THE KILL-

BOOK VII IN THE EVIL STRYKER SERIES

Cover Illustration by Linda Nilsen Worker
lindanilsenworker.com

Editing Services and Formatting: Stacey Smekofske EditsByStacey.com

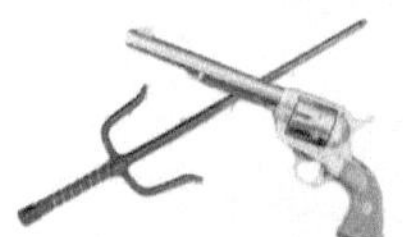

Printed in the United States of America.

ISBN Paperback: 979-8-9883083-0-0

ISBN ePub: 979-8-9883083-1-7

*To my very patient wife, Pamela, who must put up with Wes Rand.
And to my old buddies from Kingsport whom I recently reconnected with,
Jim Minnick, Pat Loven, and Tony Grills.*

Do evil men like Mao, Stalin, Hitler, and Putin ever feel remorse?
Do they simply sail through their wicked lives without any regret
for the deaths and suffering they cause?

"Art is to console those who are broken by life."

— -VINCENT VAN GOGH

CHAPTER ONE

It was the ninth of August, but you'd never know it. The cold rainy day in the Santa Cruz Mountains (a ridge separating the Pacific Ocean from the Santa Clara Valley) carried a heavy mid-afternoon fog that hovered over the ground and refused to burn off. It looked thick enough to punch through. It was not sufficiently cold enough for a snowstorm, a thermometer would read two degrees above that, but a stiff wind blowing through the pines made it bone-chillingly cold.

Rain soaked the lone rider's denims down to his boots. The devilish rain had even found its way to drip around the stained Stetson and run down his upturned collar. Both he and the big roan horse on which he rode blew vaper puffs in the heavy mist. It had been a miserable ride up to the ridgeline running from Black Mountain. He still had many more rain-soaked miles to go before he dropped off the ridgeline and reached the Southern Pacific Railroad, which would take him to San Francisco. A trip up the coast to San Francisco from Pescadero would have been on level ground, but it was much longer, and tracks had yet to be laid along the coast. Over the mountains, a shorter, albeit steeper, ride led to the train.

The rider wasn't too bothered. He'd seen worse, much worse. The many scars on his lean frame would attest to that, but the most egregious scars couldn't be seen. His parents were butchered by union thugs on San Francisco's Embarcadero when he was seven, and he once had a wife. Leigh was her name. A pretty thing, blonde hair, blue eyes. They'd married when he was still an artillery major in the Army. A firepower demonstration gone wrong ended her life, along with the rest of her immediate family. Two men had been responsible for the deaths. He'd rammed a saber through the gut of the first man, putting him on a wanted poster for murder. The second man rode the rain-soaked roan–he should have double-checked the settings on the howitzer.

He wore the guilt of a violently tragic past like a heavy overcoat. The weathered lines on his face were not laugh lines. A Colt Peacemaker .44 hung on his right hip. A .44-40 Winchester rested in the scabbard. He kept a straight razor in his back pocket he used for shaving–most of the time. But it was the weapon stuck in a pouch at the small of his back that had caused more than a few men to stare in wonderment as they watched their blood drain down its prongs. The fork-like weapon called a sai had three shiny steel tines honed to needle-point sharpness, the middle tine being longer than the other two. Normally used in pairs, he carried only one. His uncle, a master in martial arts, had taught him how to fight with it. When he'd turned fourteen, he used it to kill two sons of the Union thugs who'd murdered his parents. The boys had taken delight in regularly beating the hell out of him. On separate rainy nights, he'd gotten each one on the ground and rammed the center tine down their throats. After that, his uncle sent him east to study, which probably saved his life. He got caught up in the Civil War in his mid-teens, where he caught the eye of a general, who recommended him to the West Point Military Academy.

The man came from lines of Mexican, Asian, and European heritage– a mixed breed. A few gray strands of hair started to pepper the black hair that hung to his shoulders. Prominent facial bones above his hollow cheeks framed a week-old beard along the jawline. He wore his mustache Mexican style, drooping at the ends beneath a thin nose. His recessed steel-gray eyes sat under sharp ridges, making the ghostly orbs resemble those of a predator bird. At six feet three inches, the tall man weighed two hundred pounds, give or take a beer or two. At one time, he might have been called a handsome, dashing young officer. That's no longer true today. He's neither young nor dashing. The dress-right-dress demeanor has long since worn off, and his officer's uniform, adorned with medals, was discarded in a hotel room back east. His fierce countenance keeps most people, especially women, at bay. He's had enemies, lots of them. Most occupy graves. No one got a second chance. The name on the saddle skirt used to read in bright gold lettering, "MAJOR NEVILLE STRYKER." But heavy usage and harsh weather over the years have worn off some of the letters. Many say what's left is more fitting: "EVIL STRYKER." They say he's a ruthless killer, and few would argue.

He has no family, nor does he have anyone he'd call a friend. A U.S. senator in California named George Hearst assigned secret, personal missions to the man, missions requiring discretion and Stryker's unique skills. For those trips he was well paid; besides, he figured, he had nothing better to do. Stryker is not a man comfortable just sitting on his ass. Hearst saved his life when he'd kept a bunch of angry loggers in Felton from chopping him to death. So, there was that. In return, Stryker did get the *San Francisco Examiner* deeded over to the senator, who had won it in a poker game. Hearst wanted to give the newspaper to his son, William Randolph Hearst, but the owner was reluctant to turn it over. The recalcitrant owner did not survive the transaction. Hearst also paid Stryker one hundred thousand dollars for the job. Since then, Stryker performed other tasks for Hearst. However, there is another reason Stryker worked for the senator–a woman. Her name is Morgan Bickford. She's a mining engineer employed by Hearst. The missions for the senator also gave Stryker an excuse to see her.

Morgan's a good-looking woman, a widow. She and Stryker met in a town named Egalitaria. It used to be called Bickford before a gang of ruthless thugs killed Morgan's husband. The gang sought to enrich themselves under the political scheme of a utopian socialist system. But the gangsters made the mistake of stealing Stryker's horse, and in the process of retrieving it, he helped Morgan avenge her husband's murder. Let's just say, after a lot of bloodshed, he and the woman got what they both wanted.

In addition to Morgan's good looks–and the fact that she feels damn good under him–Stryker is attracted to her for another reason. She has philosophical principles and values he had not encountered, or even thought about before. Essentially, they are that a man has the moral right to achieve his purpose. Her bold stance and its clear logic are immensely appealing to him.

But there was a problem. The jinx. Starting at an early age at the death of his parents, everyone Stryker got close to or got close to him was killed. His wife, Leigh, and every other woman he took up with met a violent death. It made no sense. He knew that. Yet, it happened time and time again. Pavlov's dog. Eventually, Stryker reacted to the jinx. Wanting to see Morgan live meant he had to stay away from her. That was why he rested and resides in Pescadero. He only saw her on occasion. And she's remained alive.

Pescadero, a sleepy little town is about two miles from the Pacific Ocean. Isolated and ideal for a man who wants to be left alone for a while. Stryker rented a room at a boarding house, and every morning he rode to the beach and decided on whether to ride up the coast or down the coast. A trail on top of the escarpment ran along the beach, providing an easy ride with a view. When he returned to the boarding house, Elena, the owner, had breakfast ready for him. How she knew when he was returning, Stryker never asked. But breakfast, usually steak and eggs, was always hot.

Elena, in her late forties and a mixed Mexican breed like Stryker, also provided him with the latest copy of the *San Francisco Examiner* in the morning, although, it might have been a few days old. It didn't matter. She knew he especially wanted to read the *"Personals"* section. It was in that section of the paper where Hearst posted his requests for Stryker's services. The requests were written by Morgan. Reading the article was a source of relief since it also told him Morgan remained among the living. He'd found her posting in the *"Personals"* earlier that morning.

It had been a brief notice. However, those *were* Morgan's initials. Elena packed him a lunch, and he started for San Francisco right after breakfast, in a heavy downpour. By mid-afternoon, Stryker had ridden up the winding trail of Pescadero Creek Road and then on to the Alpine

Trail where he crested the last ridgeline of the Santa Cruz Mountains. He headed more southernly, along Skyline Ridge where the altitude ran between 3,300 and 3,700 ft. The fog hung below the mountain tops and the rain had let up. Below, the fog layer hovered around lower elevations, and the pine trees poked up through the fog resembling trees on a snow-covered landscape.

It was several miles before he started down the eastern slopes toward Saratoga. When he did, the fog lifted enough for tree trunks and under-growth to be visible, but for now, the tops of soaring redwoods remained enshrouded in mist. Water from the downpour ran down the trail, making footing difficult. At least the wind blew a little less on the eastern side of the mountains, but the roan was tired, slipping often. It seemed as if it was only a matter of time before it went down and sent Stryker for a spill in the mud. He needed to find dry shelter to rest and feed the horse. An abandoned toll cabin lay farther down the mountain where he normally stopped and spent the night before continuing to San Francisco. The grade leveled out and was not quite as slippery, then the cabin became the objective. Stryker reined in the roan to rest it under a redwood. He poured water from his canteen into a canvas nose bag and held it up for the horse to drink. He let it suck water for a couple of minutes before taking the bag away and dumping out the rest. He threw in some oats and strapped the bag to the roan's muzzle.

Rainwater still found its way through the coulter pine's boughs to drip on Stryker and the roan, although it was not as much as being out in the open. The redwoods on the eastern side of the mountains weren't as prevalent or as big as those closer to the coast. The coulters provided more cover anyway. He estimated it was maybe two more miles to the cabin. Remembering it had a river rock fireplace, he counted on a warm fire to dry him before riding on to Saratoga in the morning and then on over to the train in San Jose. A loafing shed stood behind the cabin as a shelter for horses, and a watering stream ran beyond it. *Let's get there.* Stryker pulled the nose bag, crammed it in the saddle bag, and climbed back in the saddle.

The rain came down harder in the open, encouraging Stryker to get to the cabin. Fog thinned somewhat (fog can be fickle), allowing him to see at least a hundred yards ahead. In another twenty minutes on the muddy trail, the cabin came into view. *Shit*. Three black buggies parked in front also came into view. No smoke rose from the chimney.

The three horses remained standing in the rain hitched to the buggies. That left plenty of room in the loafing shed for the roan. It also suggested Stryker wouldn't care for the folks inside. After watering the roan in the stream, he pulled the bridle and replaced it with a halter before hitching the horse to one of three tether rings in the shed. The shelter's wood structure showed signs of rot, but it would hold as long as the roan remained satisfied out of the rain. He wiped down the horse and then gathered up pine needles and kindling from under the shed before heading around the cabin.

As Stryker walked by the buggies, he felt nothing for the horses, but he felt disdain for people inside the cabin. He kicked open the door. He waited a moment to let his eyes adjust. The interior was damp and musty, the air hung heavy with the smothering odor of wet clothing.

Six people. None showed a weapon. Two women, four men. The women, seated at a small oak table, shrieked when the door banged open. Stryker stood in the doorway. Rain was blowing in the one-room cabin through open windows on the side walls. Whatever had provided protection from the outdoors, glass or shutters, was long gone from the openings. The men and women were clustered in the middle of the room. One man sat at the table with the women, and the other three men stood next to the table, smoking cigarettes.

"Good day, sir." The man who sat with the women extended the greeting. He wasn't smoking. The table was the only piece of furniture in the sparse cabin. A table and four chairs, that was it. It was a daytime stopover.

Stryker ignored the greeting and brushed past the standing men with cigarettes. He pulled the wet and green pine branches they'd tried to start a fire with from the fireplace and threw them on the floor. After laying the dry pine needles on the hearth, he crisscrossed the kindling he'd brought in above them on the grate. Then he struck a match to the needles.

"One of you men go outside and bring in dry branches. Get 'em under low tree cover where it's dry. Do it now," Stryker ordered with his back to them. He doffed the Stetson and gently waved it at the kindling. The nascent flame grew bigger.

The three men with the smokes took turns looking at one another. Finally, one of them said, "I'll go," and he flicked his cigarette to the floor.

Perhaps a word about leadership might be useful here. Some men are born leaders. Some are born followers. Maybe it's in the genes or jeans. It seems assumptive. There are good leaders and bad leaders, and there are good leaders who are evil. History points them out. There are followers who are led. Some want to be led. They will even follow evil leaders. History points them out too. It's puzzling though, why otherwise good citizens are willing to be led by evil monsters. Anyway, Stryker gives orders because he does. The men in the cabin obey. It's in the genes or jeans, or the Colt on Stryker's hip.

"About time someone knew how to start a damn fire!" A woman sneered.

Stryker stood, scooted a chair closer to the fire, but didn't sit. Time to take stock of the folks inside. A quick survey when he'd earlier passed them going to the fireplace told him the men posed no perceivable threat. They were unarmed. Now he stood with his back to the fire and studied the people in the room, one by one.

"Put some on the fire," Stryker told the wood fetcher who'd returned with dry branches. "Just a few and spread 'em out," he said. *How is it that grown men don't know how to start a damn fire?*

"Rain's letting up a little," the wood carrier said somewhat cheerfully.

"This is my wife, Prissy Nightingale," the man seated with the women said. "My name's Floyd Mayfield."

"My name's not Prissy," the wife, a dolled-up beauty, huffed. "It's Priscilla." Priscilla was gorgeous, getting along in years, maybe sneaking up on thirty-five, and carrying only one or two extra pounds. She had curly blonde locks and a made-up face to suffer a non-life-threatening wound for. *She wasn't to die for though. You die for your country or your family.* But still, Stryker had to admit, the woman was a beauty.

"Well, my dear, it's not Priscilla either." Floyd gave a reproachful smile to his haughty mate. "It's Ruth. Ruth Carter." He gave Stryker a grin. "She's a world-renown opera singer." Probably added that as atonement for the name revelation. "She can really belt out the high notes." More penitence.

"Can hit 'em higher if a woman takes it up the ass," Stryker said. He has a way about him. There are two situations when a man can say pretty much what he wants: when he's so old he doesn't give a shit, and when he carries a .44 and a straight razor, and he is proficient with both.

Snickers erupted from the two men standing. A sarcastic cough came from the man kneeling by the fireplace.

"And this lady is Raelyn Feeling," Floyd said, who had managed to maintain his composure, shifting the attention to the other female. Raelyn, a fetching brunette in her own right, didn't seem as haughty. "She's an actress, and so is her husband, Warren." Floyd pointed at Warren who nodded and saluted with the cigarette. "The man beside him is Wilford B. Burnside, Mayor of Saratoga," Floyd said. Wilford smiled kindly. "And Mister Fitzgerald over there by the fireplace, Frederick Fitzgerald, is a writer. We call him Fritz. He's writing the biography on Mayor Burnside." Wilford smiled kindly again.

"And who do we have to thank for building a fire for us?" Floyd asked. He acted friendly enough.

"Stryker."

"Glad to meet you, Stryker." Floyd gave a well-executed salute to his brow.

Mayor Burnside, a short, overweight man in his fifties, switched the cigarette to his left hand and extended the free hand to Stryker. He also smiled kindly. The mixed breed ignored it. Burnside withdrew the proffered hand, switched the cigarette back to his right hand, and brought it to his mouth. He took a long puff and blew it out. Then he turned to the crackling fire. "How's it coming, Fritz?"

Stryker let his eyes return to Priscilla. Yes, she was a good-looking woman even under all the war paint. Not much of the fleshy puffiness many women of the day carried. She had sharp but delicate facial bones, flashy blue eyes, and bright red cherry lips. Some women use their beauty to attract and keep a man, preferably an equally handsome man, even more preferably a handsome wealthy man. Stryker suspected Priscilla used her beauty as a weapon.

Stryker moved his eyes from the opera singer who could hit high notes and aimed them at Raelyn. At least fifteen years younger than Priscilla, she maintained a certain innocence of youth. So did her young and handsome husband with shiny black hair. Life appeared to have been pleasant for them, a rich parent maybe, or perhaps rich parents. When children are raised with money, life's hard lessons aren't learned and don't show on carefree faces. Lucky them.

Floyd was most likely wealthy to have warbling eye candy as his wife. He wasn't anywhere near handsome. He had a kind face though, and Stryker figured the man was the type who could be taken advantage of by a beautiful woman like Priscilla. *You can pull a freight train with a pussy hair.* He guessed both got what they wanted.

"The girls wanted to see the tall trees, redwoods in the Big Basin," Floyd said. "Wasn't raining when we started out this morning. Ran into the Mayor and Mister Fitzgerald on the way."

"You don't look like outdoorsmen," Stryker allowed.

"We had a guide, but his horse pulled up lame. He stayed behind and tended to it. Told us to go back the same way we came. Did okay following the trail, but this darn rain storm… well here we are for a bit." Fritz volunteered the rest of their story after rising from the fireplace and brushing his hands off on his pants. He searched his shirt pocket for the makings of another cigarette while he spoke.

"The trip was farther than I remembered. We needed a rest and so did the horses," the portly mayor added.

"The guide said it was too far to go in one day, but some of us really wanted to see the trees." Floyd dipped his head in favor of his songbird wife–who could hit high notes.

"I wasn't the only one," Priscilla claimed. "And seeing those magnificent trees was worth it, wasn't it?" She flaunted her blonde curls with her hand and glared at her husband. Then she trained her scowl at Raelyn and the three standing men. Floyd shrugged his shoulders. Raelyn smiled pleasantly. The other men weakly nodded.

Stryker turned and knelt by the fire, which was dying out. He re-positioned the logs using a dry one from the pile by the fireplace and fanned the flames again.

Behind him, the door suddenly flung open.

"Hands in the air!" Two young men and a girl rushed into the cabin. The scraggily-looking bunch came in with guns drawn. One boy was waving a Navy Colt. The other kid was skinny and tall, and he carried a .410 shotgun. The girl had a .22 long.

"Shit, it's dark in here, Heiner," the shorter boy whispered. He crowded in next to his buddy holding the revolver. The boys wore long ragged dusters, unbuttoned to show plaid shirts and denims with ropes as belts underneath.

"We've got two guns and a shotgun here!" Heiner, the tall kid, warned. "Keep 'em up! Shoot the first one that moves, Gil. Rusty, go around behind and make sure they ain't got no guns on 'em." When the girl didn't move, Heiner gave the order a second time. "Do it now, Rusty!"

The girl hesitated, then leaped in front of the boys' guns.

"No, dammit!" Heiner yelled. He grabbed Rusty's coat collar and pulled her back. "Shit, girl. Go around the table. Shoot 'em if they try anything." Whether Heiner meant what he said, one couldn't tell. He kept saying it, though.

Stryker, still kneeling, twisted around to see who was doing the yelling. The big kid, the one he figured to be Heiner, stood roughly six feet and was lanky and square-jawed. He wore his western hat slanted back on unruly blond hair. You could call him handsome. The other boy, shorter by four inches but probably weighing more than his good-looking sidekick, had a burgeoning belly. Rusty, Stryker figured was about the same age as the boys, maybe a little younger. She was pretty with red hair, freckles, and, from what he could see, good teeth. *What is it about girls, who appear to be of good stock, that makes them want to latch onto a bad seed?* Stryker wondered. *A charismatic, handsome asshole like him attracts girls like flies to shit, I reckon.*

Stryker remained crouched by the fireplace. Rusty saw him as she came from behind the two women and Floyd who were seated at the table. "There's another'n back here!"

Heiner strained his eyes to see Stryker. He punched the Colt forward, itching to fire, but he couldn't see his target. Gil waved the shotgun back and forth.

Stryker rose to his feet behind the mayor. He stood a head taller than the politician.

"He armed?" Heiner yelled.

"No." The girl had failed to notice the Peacemaker under his slicker.

Stryker guessed this was her first rodeo.

Rusty skipped the three people at the table and stepped behind Warren who was holding his hands above his head with the cigarette still burning in his fingers. She shoved the pistol barrel into his back.

"I'm not armed, miss, but the cigarette is about to burn my fingers," Warren said. "Shit!" He cursed, dropping his arm and shaking his fingers. His sudden movement startled Rusty. She pulled the trigger.

A .22 pistol is a small caliber weapon, but it can still do an awful lot of damage.

The shot—sounding more like a popgun—surprised everyone in the cabin, even Rusty.

"Oh, that's not good. That's not good at all." Warren groaned, sinking to his knees.

Stryker slipped behind Rusty, pulling the razor from his back pocket. He trapped her chin under his left forearm, dug the tip in beneath her left ear, and drew the blade across her throat. He dropped the razor, pulled the Peacemaker, and fired while he held the girl in front of him.

The first round hit Gil in the chest, left of center, and the big .44 slug blasted him back out the door where he crumpled to the ground. The shotgun fell from his grasp without firing. He lay on his side in front of the cabin, coughing up blood in the rain and died.

Heiner took the second round in his stomach, the third in his chest. He stumbled forward two steps, sprayed a welter of blood out his mouth, and triggered a wild shot in the table before falling face down on the floor. He released a groan, which sounded strangely peaceful, and then gave up the ghost.

"Warren!" Raelyn was too shocked to react at first but found her voice.

"I don't feel too good, my love." Warren attempted to get to his feet but settled back on his heels. "I heard it," he said, shaking his head. "And then something bit me. I know she shot me, though. Never knew what it would feel like." Warren kind of smiled at his wife.

"Somebody, help us!" Raelyn curled an arm around her husband's shoulders. "Please, help us!" Raelyn yelled louder, more urgently.

"Does anyone here know anything about gunshots?" Mayor Burnside roared. "Wounds, I mean," he quietly added.

Stryker swung Rusty aside, letting her fall to the floor. He stepped behind Warren and knelt. Lifting the back of his coat, he saw a fist-sized splotch of black blood mid-left on the actor's white shirt.

Raelyn gazed up at Stryker, looking hopeful.

"She got him in the liver." Stryker dropped the coattail.

"He'll be okay, won't he?"

"No."

Raelyn's hopeful countenance faded to a vacuous glare. "Warren…" she began, still looking at Stryker, "he doesn't know what he's talking about." She turned to her husband. "You'll be fine. We need to get you to a doctor, though."

Stryker got to his feet, backed up to the fire, and spread his palms behind him to warm by the blaze.

"Help me get him in the buggy, somebody." Raelyn placed her hands under Warren's armpits and attempted to lift him to his feet. The struggling woman's plea galvanized Fritz to help. He leaped on the other side of Warren, grabbed his arm, and lifted. Together, the two of them managed to get Warren on his feet. He put his arms around their shoulders and they helped him walk outside. They stepped around Gil's body at the door and got Warren in a buggy. Raelyn climbed in next to him. Fritz untied the reins and handed them to her. She pulled the horse away from the rail and snapped the leather.

Rusty's gurgling caught Mayor Burnside's attention. He hadn't moved at all. He just watched the violence. He stared at the dying girl and asked, "Did you have to kill her?"

"No." Stryker turned around and faced the fire. It was burning well, and he didn't need to add another log.

"Well, that's settled." Burnside chose not to press the matter.

"We should go too, dear," Floyd said to his wife, scooting back his chair. He helped Priscilla get up from the table.

Priscilla looked over at the mixed breed. "I hope you'll be going to San Francisco."

She got no reply.

The mayor fell in behind Floyd and Priscilla as they exited the cabin. Outside, the rain had stopped, and Stryker heard the buggies creak as everyone, including Fritz, climbed in their carriages. Then, there were a couple of "gitty-ups," sharp snaps of the reins, and they were off.

Stryker was left alone, except for the dead boys and the dying girl. He continued to warm his hands by the fire. Rusty, who lay on her back by his feet, stared blankly toward the ceiling and then stopped gurgling.

CHAPTER TWO

An hour down the road, Raelyn's buggy hit a jolting bump, and Warren groaned for the last time. After a while, Raelyn suspected her husband had died, but she didn't stop. That would've taken precious time, wasted time, if he still lived, and by not stopping, she delayed confirmation of his death. A half-hour later, she got confirmation in Saratoga.

Stryker hung around the cabin for another hour, warming himself by the fire. He made a hot cup of coffee shortly after the others left. He only heated one cup of the brew since none of the other three in the cabin acted like they wanted any. Streaks of sunlight began to appear through the trees, and he allowed the cabin would soon warm, hastening the stench of the dead. The flies would be arriving before long to drop their maggots. After briefly considering using the roan to pull the bodies out and away from the cabin, he nixed it. The rain had stopped, and it was maybe two more hours to Saratoga, a hotel room, and a warm bed. He could've spent the night by the fire with the bodies piled up in a corner. He nixed that too. Not that he couldn't stomach the dead, he'd seen plenty of dead in the war; he'd spent nights on the battlefield with them. Some weren't quite dead, and they moaned or cried all night. He'd seen lots of dead after the war, too, many killed by his own hand. Truthfully, he just didn't want the bodies and their flies to ruin his breakfast.

Stryker threw on his coat, gathered up the coffee, the pot, and the cup, and loaded them in the saddlebags. He climbed on the roan and headed down the trail to Saratoga, leaving Heiner, Gil, and Rusty to the flies.

The sun's warmth caused clouds of steam to rise from the open ground, and as Stryker rode lower down the mountain, the mist grew heavier, reminding him of a low-level bog. The surrounding landscape turned eerie. Stryker couldn't see beyond a few dozen feet, and animals that were invisible in the fog moved in the brush. Smaller varmints scurried among the undergrowth and pine needles. Larger animals, prey or predators, Stryker couldn't tell which, moved through the brush unseen. The roan acted skittish. Black bears and the fierce grizzly roamed throughout the Santa Cruz Mountains. Stryker rode with his hand draped over the Peacemaker.

No Mister Mayor, I didn't have to kill her. I probably didn't have to kill any of them. I could have held the blade to her throat and threatened to kill her unless the boys laid down their guns, or left. So why then, Stryker asked himself. He already knew the answer. No need to think about it. No need to second guess. It took years, years of a relentlessly violent life. A relentless series of threats and attacks—then in the war, all the bloody battles. Since he'd seen his parents killed when he was seven, since he'd been bullied by older kids, since he got caught up in a senseless war at age fourteen, since the brutal Indian campaigns—since he'd accidentally killed his wife. After her death, it's been one God-damn tragic loss after another. Anyone who gets close dies. His jinx.

All these past events shaped him, made him who he is. To survive, there could have been no other outcome. He'd become like a mongrel dog beaten all its life. When cornered or threatened, it reacts savagely with slashing teeth, turned vicious it will kill without forethought. So, Stryker doesn't plan his reactions. He doesn't think things out. His mind plays no part in a violent reply. Those who have the misfortune to cross him usually end up dead.

As the road leveled out at lower elevations, Stryker noticed it was turning into a nice evening. His right arm hung freely at his side; his hand no longer on the walnut butt of the Colt. He'd ridden the road (that no longer charged twenty-five cents toll) to the Southern Pacific depot in Saratoga many times, and he knew the little picturesque town to be not much farther. The sun had long disappeared below the mountains behind him and took its shadows with it. It would be pitch black soon. He was bone tired, and if the roan could talk, he would probably grumble the same thing. The big horse must have sensed rest and food lay just ahead because it picked up speed. Stryker looped the reins around the saddle horn and let it set its own pace. He couldn't see the road very well anyway.

Rounding a heavily forested hillock, he emerged on the crest of a sparsely wooded slope, sweeping down to a broad valley where the lights of the Pacific Congress Springs Hotel came into view. The last time Stryker traveled through Saratoga, he spent the night there. Trips before the last year he camped in the mountains and then had ridden through to San Jose before boarding the train for San Francisco. This night, he allowed the Springs Hotel resort to be a reward for the hard ride across the Santa Cruz Mountains. The rain and unwelcome company in the toll cabin—and the dead left inside—urged him to stop in Saratoga. Hearst can wait a day or two.

Big Basin Road wound its way down and morphed into the wider Congress Springs Road. The Congress Springs Resort on the west end of Saratoga was a popular vacation spot. A sprawling two-story wooden complex sat on 720 acres. Its white paint with green trim boasted private rooms and cottages, hot baths from the natural springs, and lush grounds for picnicking. One could fish nearby at Quito Creek with its abundant trout, and there were groomed hiking trails for guests. It even had its own dairy and winery. Yes, the Pacific Congress Springs Resort was the place to be for the wealthy, fashionable, and elite. Of course, the rough-dressed man on the roan would fit right in.

Stryker stabled the roan, paid seventy-five cents for its groom and feed, grabbed his saddlebags, and made his way to the front desk to get a room. They gave him a cottage, the last one in its row, far away from the center of activity. He didn't even have to ask for it. He withdrew a clean shirt, underwear, and dungarees from the saddlebags, and headed for a short washup in the hot mineral springs bathhouse. A quick one; he was doing a hungry belly's bidding. He dropped off the dirty clothing in the cottage and set about getting something to eat. An A-frame sign by the La Sage Hall door read in big letters "Welcome Western Mining Association," and in smaller block letters below that was "Other Guests Welcome." The Hall was used for conferences and dining as well. Being well past nine o'clock, he grunted his surprise to find the restaurant still open. Not only was it open, but it was also filled with a bustling crowd, eating and drinking–well, mostly drinking now–and being pretty raucous. At the north end of the room was a two-foot stage with a piano and a female singer. The blonde-headed warbler was drowned out by the boisterous crowd. Floyd, who sat at the piano, accompanied his wife, Pricilla, by banging out a lively tune. No opera tonight. She laughed and cavorted about the stage, sashaying with her skirt and enjoying the frivolous atmosphere.

Stryker saw a waiter wearing a white jacket and grabbed him by the upper arm. "Bring me some food." The man started to protest. Stryker tightened his grip. "Make it hot. I don't care what it is," Stryker growled.

"Well, there's stew. Still on the stove."

"And a beer," Stryker said, scanning the room. He failed to find Mayor Burnside and Fritz seated anywhere, nor Raelyn. He didn't expect her to be enjoying the evening with this crowd.

Stryker spotted a small table for two in the corner. "I'll be over there." He canted the Stetson toward it and released the waiter's arm. The man spun around and headed to the kitchen, rubbing his sore bicep.

The Congress Springs Hotel was nowhere near the opulence of San Francisco's Palace Hotel. The Palace stood eight stories high, the Congress Springs only two stories. Stryker liked this place better. No brass rails, no polished marble, no baths in each room, no rising room (elevator), and it missed lots of other elements of luxurious comfort, but he still preferred the Springs Resort. The Palace was too damn stuffy.

Large enough to easily hold 100 people, twenty-five tables, four to a table, the La Sage Hall was close to full capacity. Painted white with green trim, same as the outside walls, it had a walnut planed floor, white linen tablecloths, kerosene lanterns on the walls, candles on the tables, and the stage in front where Priscilla pranced. Shouted orders and rattling pots and pans escaped above the kitchen's batwing doors left of the main entrance and near Stryker's table. Not the best seat in the house, but he wasn't there for the entertainment.

The beer arrived first, cold and in a frosty mug. He blew off the froth, took a long drink, and watched the stage show. Priscilla sang and danced so well, one had to wonder why she bothered with opera. Priscilla finished the song and bowed to the clapping crowd that got louder with each bow. After four curtsies, she stopped and pointed to her husband. Floyd rose from the piano and took his one bow. Clapping for him quickly died off and became sporadic. The waiter brought the bowl of stew on a tray, and Stryker shifted his attention.

Floyd stood at the stage edge and thanked the audience. Priscilla slipped quietly from the platform. Floyd stayed on, announcing they couldn't perform again the next night for they were headed to San Francisco in the morning.

Stryker didn't pay attention to Floyd's remarks. Loud groans from the diners drowned out much of what he said anyway.

The stew was hot; the beef was only a little chewy. The carrots, tomatoes, potatoes, and onions were heavily spiced with salt and pepper, the way Stryker liked them. He'd eaten half the bowl's contents before he resumed gazing about the room. That's when he noticed Priscilla and Floyd hadn't left the dining hall after all. The songbird apparently couldn't get enough adulation and was flitting from table to table with Floyd tagging along beside her, or more often, behind her. Then Stryker ruefully realized, the two of them would probably see him and interrupt his meal, and they did.

"Stryker!" Priscilla was two tables away. The songstress, talking with a vertically challenged fat man, glanced over his shoulder and spotted Stryker. He had a spoonful of stew inches from his mouth. After a second's pause in flight, the spoon continued without acknowledging Priscilla's greeting. But the damn woman grabbed Floyd's arm and dragged her husband around the fat man to Stryker's table.

"Didn't expect to see you here!" Priscilla said. What she meant by that was the Congress Springs Hotel was too upscale for him. She seemed to not notice his clean shirt.

Stryker slammed the empty spoon on the table linen with an irritable thud. "All right, sit down!" If she sat and lowered her voice, maybe the diners nearby would quit staring at him. Most of them did when she lowered her shapely figure into the chair across from him. Floyd pulled an empty chair from a nearby table and sat as well.

"You're staying here at the resort?" She asked, not entirely able to hide her skepticism.

Stryker thought about saying no, but she might catch him in the lie sometime later, maybe at breakfast. The mixed breed may be a ruthless killer, but he's generally truthful. "Yes."

Priscilla remained quiet for a moment, perhaps trying to think of something to make up for the implied insults.

Floyd stepped in to help her out. "It's a pleasant surprise." He *had* noticed the clean shirt. "Obviously he does dear, can't you see, Mister Stryker's all cleaned up," Floyd said, without any hint of sarcasm.

"It's good to see you," Priscilla said with a smile bordering on fake. "Are you going on to San Francisco in the morning as well?"

Stryker wiped his mouth with a napkin. "Yes."

"That's fine." Priscilla leaned closer and lowered her voice. "Let's put that awful mess at the cabin behind us, shall we?" She straightened. The hint of a smile remained. She waited for Stryker to acknowledge her request.

For some reason, that didn't sit well with him. "Stew's getting cold. Leave."

Priscilla reared back. Shocked, her eyes grew wider and her eyebrows arched skyward. The nascent smile vanished.

"Let's go, dear," Floyd said. He got to his feet and stepped behind Priscilla's chair.

She looked as if she intended to respond with a scathing riposte, but Stryker's steely-eyed stare narrowed. Multiple thoughts undoubtedly streaked through Priscilla's brain–like remembering he *was* a vicious killer. She held her tongue. She stood and allowed Floyd to scoot back her chair.

"Have a pleasant evening, sir," Floyd said, taking Priscilla's arm, and nodding to Stryker.

Stryker picked up the spoon, slanted the bowl toward him, and ladled a full load of stew. It was still kind of warm, and he spooned out the rest of the stew before he washed down the last bite with a mouthful of beer.

Floyd and Priscilla let Stryker's table be the last to visit. They quickly exited the dining room, ignoring entreaties by other conferees and guests to stop and chat.

After draining the last of the beer, Stryker headed back to his room. He threw off his clean outfit and fell into bed, exhausted. He was so tired, a nightmare about Leigh didn't hit him until right before daybreak.

Another horrific dream of his dead wife haunted his sleep. He despised the damn things, yet they did allow him to see Leigh again. Sure, she had visited in his sleep, but ghoulishly. Leigh always appeared bloodied and disfigured. The dreams tormented the man, leaving him torn between joy and anguish and crushing melancholy. Tonight was no different.

The day Leigh was killed, the artillery round had exploded in a picturesque meadow where she and her family picnicked, far outside the targeted impact area. The settings on the howitzer had been changed, changed to make Stryker, a weapons analyst for the investment banking firm of James P. Morgan, fail in the firepower demonstration for Volker Munitions. Volker planned an initial public stock offering three months later. A competing firm planned its offering five months later. An agent of the competitor switched the firing coordinates on the adjusting howitzer. The malevolent agent died; he was impaled to a wall with a saber rammed through his liver. His murder had made Stryker a wanted man.

Stryker could handle most adversities with gun and blade, but not the nightmares. This one began like many others, with him finding Leigh's broken body on the ground, bleeding from multiple shrapnel wounds. Her white dress was blackened with gunpowder. He rushed to her side and lifted her head. Leigh opened her eyes, that being the last time he saw how sparkling blue they were. She'd said his name on the blood flowing from her mouth before she died.

That's how Stryker remembers his wife. The image of her death burned into his brain, blacking out memories of the fun times when they laughed and enjoyed life.

Tonight, she died in his arms again, like so many times before. Then, a new scene appeared, one he'd not had in prior nightmares. Her body rose from the bare dirt exposed by the explosion, and became upright, hovering two feet above the ground and some distance away from him. Her spirit?

"I loved you so, and you killed me." Leigh talked without moving her lips the way a person does in dreams. "Why did you do it?" She cried.

"I should have checked the settings, Leigh." He tried to stand but he couldn't make his legs work. He got up to all fours and tried to crawl, but it was like crawling through quicksand. Dreams do that to you, you know. You try to run from something, or run toward it, and you can't move. He couldn't have gotten to her anyway. She floated away, growing smaller as she drifted off across the field.

"Wait, Leigh!" He pushed harder. No good. "Leigh!"

There was more cannon fire. He heard it pounding to his left. "God, don't let it hit her again! God!" Stryker yelled. *Did I just hear myself scream that?*

The pounding turned into heavy rapping on the door. "Stryker? You all right?" The door swung open. Priscilla and Floyd Nightingale stood staring at the man on all fours, wearing his red long johns, rocking back and forth on the floor.

It took another two seconds for Stryker to regain total consciousness. He finally became fully awake and cursed himself for not immediately being alert. In the army, he'd learned to doze with part of his brain still active, able to sense danger. It didn't happen this time. His brain wasn't programmed to warn him of impending embarrassments. Not a propitious moment.

"Go away, dammit!" Stryker jumped to his feet. The long johns were actually his summer short johns. They had the legs cut off above the knee. He took two steps toward the Nightingales and slammed the door shut. He was pulling on his denims when the door opened again.

"I need your help." Priscilla looked as if she'd just rolled out of bed, detectable by her unkempt hair, no war paint on her face, and lips a natural color instead of cherry red. Stryker thought she looked better that way. She marched into the room with Floyd in tow. Priscilla positioned herself in the center of the room, facing Stryker who was standing and buckling his belt. He sat back on the bed to pull on his boots.

"Raelyn's disappeared," Priscilla announced. She watched Stryker pull on his boots and then reach for his shirt before continuing. "We think she's been kidnapped and is in danger."

"None of my business," Stryker growled. *Been better if Floyd caught me fucking his damn wife. Shit.*

"She's my business. Raelyn's my sister, and you're gonna help me get her back."

Stryker sat on the bed, eying the woman as he buttoned his shirt. "Like I said, lady, none of my–"

"People here in the hotel…" Priscilla interrupted, "Or on the train, if you take it, are all gonna laugh pretty hard when they hear about a man who crawls around a room, crying in his underwear." A wry smile crept on her face, a sarcastic expression laced with pity.

Stryker thought about killing them both. He was still trying to decide how he'd do it when Priscilla added, "I'm desperate, Stryker. You gonna help me or not?"

Not because of her threat, it wasn't needed, not even to reestablish his manhood, that didn't matter, but the nightmare made him look foolish in his own eyes. It was as if he'd looked in the room and saw himself crawling on the floor. Disgusting. He had to put that picture behind him, somehow.

"Where's your sister, dammit?" Stryker asked, standing and strapping on his gun belt. He gave a hard slap on the leather to finish driving the belt through the buckle.

"We're not sure," Floyd said, stepping beside his wife. "She wasn't in her room all night. We asked some of the hotel staff, and one said he saw her out walking alone on resort property." Floyd hooked a thumb over his shoulder.

Stryker glanced up as he looped the holster string around his thigh and saw Floyd pointing. "Show me outside."

"The man said there are three Indian tipis off property in the trees near where she was headed," Priscilla said. "She could be with Indians for God's sake! But since they're not on hotel property, the hotel won't help!" Priscilla violently nodded up and down on the last three words.

"We asked management to send men over and look for her," Floyd added. "They won't go off property. So, I told Priscilla we should come find you. Sorry, we had to wake you, Stryker."

Stryker leaned down to his saddle resting on the floor and pulled the Winchester from the scabbard. "All right, let's go."

Adding to Stryker's irritation, as they walked from the room and down the hallway to the front entrance, was the enticing smell of freshly brewed coffee. He wasn't going to have any. *Bullshit!*

"Stryker! Where you going?" Priscilla yelled.

Stryker had peeled off from following Floyd and Priscilla and headed into the dining room. Priscilla ran to catch up to him with Floyd trailing behind. Floyd walked instead of running. Ten or twelve early risers for breakfast were grouped in twos or threes, already seated at tables. Stryker snatched a mug of coffee off a waiter's tray as Priscilla and Floyd rushed to him.

"Stryker…?" Priscilla began.

"Put it on their bill," Stryker told the startled waiter.

As Stryker walked away, he heard Floyd tell the waiter their room number. Husband and wife quick-stepped to catch up to Stryker and all three continued down the hallway. Once outside, Floyd pointed right and said, "This way 'round back." Floyd and Priscilla set off at a brisk pace, almost in step with one another, and Stryker trundled along behind them, resting the carbine canted on his shoulder and sipping his coffee.

Every so often, the Nightingales paused and turned around to make sure he was still following. "A recalcitrant fellow, that one," Floyd grumbled to Priscilla. He didn't seem too concerned if Stryker heard him. Stryker took it as a compliment anyway.

It was a good quarter mile across the grassy meadow to the woods. Early morning dew still lay on the six-inch grass, soaking the boots and pant cuffs of the men. Priscilla wore her stage shoes and dress; the dew dampened her shoes, ankles, and the bottom of her dress. Behind them sat the white wooden Congress Springs Hotel in the growing distance, picturesque and in sharp contrast to the lush green grass. None of the three people trudging toward the tipis in the conifers paused to look back and view the attractive setting.

Stryker picked up his pace and closed the gap between him and the Nightingales. The mug being half full was less likely to slosh out coffee.

The three tipis weren't very big. Certainly not large enough to house an Indian brave's ponies on frigid wintery nights when a respectable warrior would sometimes move his wife or wives outside to make room for his horses–even though the women almost always built the tipis. A rich brave with much honor often had more than one wife. Maybe wives were easier to replace than horses. However, these three tipis did not appear to be built by squaws, or even Indians at all. They weren't constructed out of animal hides sewn together with sinew. These tipis were made with canvas and thread. Stryker didn't know how the Nightingales felt, but he suspected they would not find Indians inside the tipis.

The sizable campfire in the middle of the three tipis smoldered. Smoke drifted upward and dispersed among the overhanging tree branches.

Stryker eased the carbine from his shoulder and cradled it in the crook of his arm, holding the last of the coffee. Other than the sound of a man softly snoring in one of the tipis and a few song sparrows chirping "good mornings" to each other, not much was happening here. The sun had risen high enough to cast their shadows on the outside canvas of the closest tipi. Stryker wondered if anyone inside had noticed.

"Good morning?" Priscilla announced, pleasantly. No reply.

Priscilla looked at Floyd and then at the impassive Stryker, who was scanning the woods around and in the back of the tipis. She nodded sideways toward the tipis for Stryker to do something. He finished off the coffee, slid the gun barrel down his forearm to his hand, and held the front stock with the coffee cup dangling off a finger.

Priscilla, frustrated by the two men, yelled out "Hello? Anybody in there?"

Stryker wasn't just being obstinate. He figured a female, rather than a male, calling out a greeting to a surprised occupant was less likely to come out shooting.

"Who's there?" Came a reply from one of the tipis. It was a man's voice, a little shaky, and none too gruff. The fellow sounded right cheerful.

"It's Priscilla. I've come for my sister, Raelyn." Priscilla took a chance.

"Priscilla?" Raelyn called from the same tipi.

Before Priscilla could fumble out the right words to draw her sister outside, the flap flung open, and Raelyn came bounding out, fully clothed. "Hello, everybody!"

"Raelyn? What are you doing out here?" Priscilla asked. The hesitant smile she gave her sister portended joy and confusion.

The tipi flap was pulled back again, more gently this time, and a man and woman stepped out. They wore white flowing robes. Flaps on the other tipi's opened and two more couples emerged, dressed the same way, in white robes.

"I've met new friends," Raelyn beamed.

Stryker expected a much younger lot to be occupying the tipis, seeking the meaning of life, perhaps. *If these couples were indeed on a like quest, it had taken them a long time to achieve the holy grail of knowledge,* he mused. These three couples were ancient. New friends of Raelyn maybe, but they were old new friends, very old. So old, in fact, Stryker wondered how they even erected the tipis. He released the front of the Winchester and held it pointed toward the ground.

"Any more in the tipi?" Stryker asked.

"No," said the old man who'd followed Raelyn outside. "It's just us. How are you this morning?"

"We're fine," Floyd spoke up. He figured Stryker had his concerns allayed, and Priscilla seemed at a loss for words.

"Who built the tents?" Stryker continued eyeing the surrounding area.

"Ohlone Indians. My name's Brother Earnest." Brother Earnest held out his hand to Floyd, and they shook hands. "My wife, Ruth." Ruth nodded at Floyd. "Used to make 'em out of bark off the Redwoods,"

Brother Earnest explained. "But now they use Levi canvas on the few they still build. Reckon it's easier than skinnin' tree bark. Don't hav'ta clean ole man Levi. He does the skinnin'." A wry smile crept onto the face of Brother Earnest.

"Raelyn, why…?" Priscilla laid her hands on her sister's shoulders, gentle-like, not reproachful.

"I was–"

"She came out here walkin' with a loaded pistol," Brother Earnest supplied.

"A loaded pistol?" Priscilla shrilled.

"I wasn't gonna shoot anybody," Raelyn said defensively, arching her eyebrows.

"We were afraid she might harm herself," Ruth, the wife of Brother Earnest interjected.

"Where's the gun?" Floyd asked what Stryker was thinking.

"We have it in there." Brother Earnest swung his hand toward the tipi. "Raelyn was very distraught last night. We stayed up late, sitting by the fire, talking. She's suffered a tragic loss, one that a girl so young should never have to endure." Brother Earnest brought his arm around Raelyn's shoulders. "However, with the good Lord's help, she'll come to realize–indeed to know–that separation from her husband, Warren, is only temporary. She'll see him again, and they'll have everlasting joy together." Brother Earnest smiled kindly at Raelyn. "Until then, Raelyn must live a righteous life, doing good, helping others. That is what we, as disciples in *The Church of The Guiding Light* do. It has filled our hearts with love now that Raelyn has decided to stay here and join together with us in our spiritual calling." Brother Earnest squeezed Raelyn's shoulder.

Raelyn offered a fractured smile.

"I'm sure you all mean well, but this fellow…" Priscilla nodded rearward, "Will fill your hearts with lead if she doesn't leave with us."

Stryker didn't know if she was joking or not.

"Com'on Raelyn." Floyd stepped up and brushed the old man's arm off Raelyn. He wrapped his arm around the girl and pulled her next to Priscilla.

"Go with them," Brother Earnest said, extending a warm and kindly countenance to Raelyn. He clasped his hands together and dipped his head. "We will pray for you."

Stryker studied the three couples and wondered if their advanced age had something to do with being so religious, *Nearer My God to Thee* since they were in the latter years. He even guessed he might be too when he got to their age, but then he realized he probably wouldn't live that long.

"They were very nice," Raelyn said as she walked beside her sister back to the hotel. Priscilla kept her arm around her. Floyd and Stryker trailed along behind. "They gave me comfort," Raelyn continued, and then she grew quiet. About halfway across the open meadow to the resort, Raelyn began to quietly sniffle. Two crows squawked overhead, and that was the only conversation to be had until they reached the hotel.

Stryker would have liked to have known where Raelyn got the pistol, but he didn't bring it up and no one else did either. He suspected she stole it.

When they climbed the steps into the resort's entrance, Stryker turned left; the others went right. There were no salutations. He stopped briefly at the front desk to check out and then went to the dining hall to refill the mug. He didn't feel like eating breakfast. The coffee would do. He walked to his room where he poured water from a pitcher into the porcelain wash basin and lathered his soap bar. After washing his face, he pulled the razor from his rear pocket and shaved, leaving the mustache intact and a little stubble along the jaw lines. After packing his carry bag, he took another sip of the coffee, sat the mug by the sink, and picked up his bag and saddle.

Down the hall, he passed the La Sage dining room and glanced in at the conferees enjoying breakfast. He walked a few steps, stopped, and turned around. Then went back. Standing in the doorway, holding the carry bag and the saddle slung over his shoulder, he took a longer look. The room bustled with chatter and waiters scurrying about, some carried trays laden with loaded breakfast plates over their shoulders while others carried empty trays under an arm as they headed to the kitchen. Newspapers were at each place setting on the tables. A few diners read the papers while others were engaged in conversations, some serious and some lighthearted. Most of the men wore suits, and those few who didn't have on a suit were still nattily dressed in string ties or stylish handkerchiefs about their necks. There were maybe ten women. They wore dresses, and Stryker figured they were wives or just *friends* of wealthy miners. But there at a far table up against the right wall, pushed near the edge of the two-foot stage, sat Floyd, Priscilla, Raelyn, and… Morgan. She had just turned to speak to Floyd when Stryker recognized her. *Morgan! What was she doing here?*

Stryker dropped the bag. He heaved the saddle off his shoulder and left it in the hall. He stepped inside. The four at the far table had yet to see him, and the other diners only gave him passing glances as he made his way across the floor through the crowded tables. Talk died down.

He came within a few feet before anyone at the table noticed him. Priscilla was the only one facing him. Floyd and Raelyn were across from each other, seated sideways to the approaching Stryker. Morgan had her back to him. Priscilla saw Stryker first. Her face brightened with cheerful recognition.

"Stryker!" Priscilla blurted a thrilled greeting. Morgan swiveled around to face him. Raelyn and Floyd turned more casually. "We were just talking about you!" Priscilla exclaimed as Stryker approached the table. "Have some coffee?" She pointed to a silver pitcher with three over-turned cups on the table. Floyd and Priscilla had coffee cups next to their breakfast plates. Glasses with orange juice and water waited in front of Morgan and Raelyn.

Stryker ignored Priscilla. He remained standing since there were no empty chairs at their table or nearby. He was most likely the only armed man in the crowded room. There may have been concealed weapons on some diners, but none wore a .44 on his hip as conspicuously as he did. The dining room's talk level remained at a low murmur, and he might have felt awkward or out of place if he hadn't been so focused on Morgan.

Her shoulder-length brunette hair hung straight and parted on one side. Dark, intelligent eyes sat above sharp cheekbones. She was thin, but not skinny, and wore little or no makeup. She was dressed in tan slacks and a white cotton shirt turned up at the collar. She gave him a warm smile, signaling the room chatter to resume, and then a speaker on the stage interrupted the conversations.

"Good morning, ladies and gentlemen." A short, portly man with struggling jacket buttons on his brown suit stood in the center of the stage and loudly announced the greeting. Table conversations simmered down to only a few who kept up their chatter. The speaker repeated his greeting more forcibly. "Good morning!" The room quieted.

"Thank you all for attending the Annual Western Miners Conference. My name is Thaddeus Hornsby, and I'll be your guest host for this two-day convention." The room erupted in loud clapping.

Stryker stepped around Morgan's chair and stood next to the wall.

"We have several knowledgeable and exciting speakers for you," Hornsby continued, "and you will be sure to take much of what you'll learn here home with you. Now the scheduling. Today's classes will end at noon, so you can have the afternoon to enjoy the fishing, hiking, sight-seeing, and of course, the spa's mineral waters. Meet back here at six o'clock for dinner. And then tomorrow we'll pick back up with classes starting at eight o'clock. The conference will conclude at noon. Now for our first speaker. After graduating at the top of her class from the Colorado School of Mines, she ran her own very successful mine in California before Senator George Hearst lured her away to be the chief mining engineer for Hearst Mining Corporation. She's applied her skills in Angel's Camp, California, Nevada in the Comstock Lode, and in Park City, Utah, for the senator. And you all know how wealthy George has become over the last few years."

Stryker knew Hornsby was talking about Morgan.

"Let's give a big round of applause for Miss Morgan Bickford!" Hornsby shouted.

Morgan looked at Stryker and mouthed, "Wait for me." She took another spoonful of oatmeal, a sip of juice, and made to shove away from the table. Stryker eased behind and scraped her chair back. Morgan rose, made the short trip from her table to the stage, and climbed up its three narrow steps.

"Stryker, take her chair and listen to her talk," Priscilla called to him above the applause.

Stryker sat and turned to watch Morgan. He'd never known Morgan gave speeches; he had never heard her talk in front of a crowd except for that time in Bickford[1].

As the applause died down, Raelyn leaned toward him and said, "Morgan told us you'd lost your wife."

Stryker jerked around his head, his face inches from Raelyn's.

"Said you had nightmares," she added.

Stryker glanced at Floyd and Priscilla. It was obvious they'd heard what Raelyn said. They looked at him with consoling expressions. That could have made him feel better, explaining why he crawled on the floor when they came to his room. It didn't though. He felt as if the three of them looked at him now, and he was naked.

He made the nine o'clock train to San Jose. He'd gotten up and left immediately, walking out of the conference as Morgan began her speech. The last words he heard were: "Even if you hit the big bonanza, you still have to work the lode, Neville." She'd seen him leave, of course. He shouldered his saddle, picked up the carpet bag, and walked out of the hotel.

It was five minutes to the stable. It took him another ten minutes to saddle the roan, and fifteen more to ride to the station. At a quarter to nine, he was on the train, seated at the rear of the coach, back against the wall, watching out the window and thinking about what made him leave. He didn't want their God-damned pity.

Back at the La Sage Hall, Morgan finished her speech an hour later. Hornsby announced a fifteen-minute break, probably thinking a break was needed. The waiters had poured a lot of coffee.

Morgan returned to the table with Floyd, Priscilla, and Raelyn.

"The man has manners?" Priscilla asked, presumably referring to Stryker pulling out Morgan's chair. Raelyn and Floyd cocked heads at Morgan too.

"Army Major. Why'd he leave?" Morgan asked.

Floyd and Priscilla turned to Raelyn.

Morgan too, and she asked, "Raelyn?"

"I just said we'd heard he lost his wife, and he had nightmares," Raelyn said, sounding defensive.

"How do you know his nightmares are about his wife, anyway, Morgan?" Priscilla wanted to know.

"I've slept with him."

CHAPTER THREE

he Southern Pacific rails from Saratoga to San Jose lay twelve miles over meadow land used by mission clergy, who grazed cattle in the valley. Stryker saw a few willow groves and an occasional oak from the train window, but most of the ground lay covered in ryegrass. The tracks crossed Tito Creek, or Saratoga Creek as it was later called. During the summer, his horseback ride to San Jose was fairly straight; in the winter months, he had to navigate around the flooded lowlands. The railroad made the trip much more comfortable for Stryker and the big roan horse that was comfortably munching on oats in the cattle car behind him.

No more than nine or ten passengers boarded the train for the trip to San Jose. He reasoned those who boarded the coach weren't part of the conference. Those who did climb on afforded him plenty of space by occupying seats near the front of the coach. Just as well, Stryker was in no mood for introductions or engaging in small talk. Gazing out the window, he had to admit there was another reason he bolted from the La Sage Hall. It lay dormant in the conference room, only now boiling to the surface. He realized the setting reminded him of the conferences he'd attended with Leigh. Working with the House of Morgan, James Pierpont Morgan's investment firm, he'd gone to many similar meetings at fancy resorts back East where he had taken his wife. The conference this morning provoked a stark reminder she wasn't with him anymore and never would be. He hated how those reminders, big and small, came back to haunt him. *Won't the damn things ever stop popping up? No, they won't.* Maybe he didn't want them to.

Stryker stopped looking out the window and shifted his attention to the other passengers. He'd made a quick evaluation when they'd boarded. There were three elderly couples and three single men who appeared middle-aged. All were well dressed in suits and top hats on the men and fancy dresses with bustles on the women. No perceived threat among them. He counted nine, and none paid him any attention after they sat. Normal well-to-do people, living well-to-do lives, that's how he judged them. No problems, no worries. Good for them. He turned back to gaze out the window. San Jose came into sight. He'd have a brief stopover before catching the 10:20 Southern Pacific to San Francisco. *What the hell did Hearst need this time?*

The 10:20 left on time, and the two passenger coaches were nearly filled to capacity. Stryker managed to settle into his customary seat on the last bench of the car, facing forward, his back against the rear wall. He had company. A shabbily dressed man in a rumpled suit sat next to him and read his newspaper aloud. Two elderly, plain-looking women with tight hair buns, spinsters perhaps, were seated across from them. The women carried on a casual conversation with each other, suggesting they might be related or maybe close friends. One pulled reading glasses and a book from her cloth satchel and began to read. The other woman withdrew needle and yarn from her carry bag and set about knitting. Stryker stretched out his long legs and pulled the brim of his Stetson down over his brow. Mumbled reading by the man next to him and the clacking train wheels prompted Stryker to doze.

The Southern Pacific made three stops on the trip to San Francisco, Palo Alto, Redwood City, and San Mateo. A few passengers got off; a few got on, but Stryker kept the Stetson lowered, alertly listening during the stopovers while not inviting conversation.

It was half-past two in the afternoon when the train rolled up to the Ferry House in San Francisco. Stryker got off, paid the ostler boy to stable the roan, and hopped on the Market Street cable car to the Palace Hotel.

Originally, the Palace Hotel was a joint venture between William Sharon and William Ralston. It was a five-million-dollar project financed with Sharon's Comstock earnings and Ralston's multi-faceted and over-leveraged business conglomerates, which included the Bank of California. Ralston assumed its construction and spared no expense in building the most fabulous hotel in the country, if not in the world, at that time. Located on the corner of Market and New Montgomery Streets, the Palace rose to a height of eight glorious stories, including the ground floor. Open in the center with a skylighted dome, each surrounding floor had white columns on balconies overlooking the grand carriage entrance below for the rich and famous.

All the 750 guest rooms had their own toilets, baths, fireplaces, and bay windows to look out over the city or panoramic views of San Francisco Bay. Redwood paneled elevators, called rising rooms, carried guests up to their rooms. The magnificent lobby was adorned with the finest teak and mahogany wood. Ornamental brass, polished daily, trimmed the dark wood. Giant potted ferns were abundantly situated in the grand entrance, lobby, and entertainment halls. There was a ladies' grille room and an even grander men's grille room next to the billiard parlor. The men's grille room also had curtained booths for gentlemen to discreetly entertain lady friends. The gentlemen's bar with all its wood, brass, and mirrors was without equal in the world. Yes, William Chapman Ralston was building a truly magnificent edifice to symbolize west coast wealth. He went bankrupt two years before it was completed. He had sold out his half of the hotel to Sharon. They found Ralston's body floating in San Francisco Bay on the same day he lost ownership of the Bank of California. Sharon finished the construction of the Palace.

Unawed, Stryker stepped into the elegant carriage entrance. The large roundabout capped with a glass dome seven stories overhead was lost on him. He held the hotel's splendid surroundings with low esteem. With well-worn denims and the imposing .44 slung on his hip, he was hardly overdressed. But Stryker was not a poor man. He had over one hundred thousand dollars in the bank, earned from Senator Hearst when he procured ownership of the *San Francisco Examiner* for Hearst's son, William Randolph. The closest thing to formal attire he'd worn was his dress-blue Army uniform more than two decades ago, and he had no suit hanging in the closet. He walked from the carriage entrance, paying no attention to the white ornate columns on each level overhead. He also ignored the multiple eight-foot potted ferns and strode his dirty boots across the marble lobby floor to the enormous mahogany desk. The towering baroque counter rose over seven-feet high, but it did have a chest-level middle section, behind which uniformed desk clerks greeted guests. Stryker approached the counter in a foul mood.

"Welcome back, Mister Stryker," the male hotel attaché said, with a broad smile. He knew the drill.

"Here to see Hearst," Stryker said.

"Of course, sir. Just a moment while I ring him." The clerk leaned to his right and pressed a call button. A couple of seconds later he spoke in the speaking tube, "Mister Stryker for you, sir." Stryker couldn't hear the muffled reply; however, the clerk straightened and told him, "Senator Hearst said to go right up, sir, and here's your room key." The senator always provided a room for him while he was in town.

Stryker headed across the spacious lobby toward the rising room, ignoring scornful glances from the other guests. No one said anything to him. The .44 and the fierce countenance on his brooding face possibly curtailed criticism.

The elevator operator greeted Stryker with a nod and closed the expandable gate before other guests could step inside. The operator obviously wanted to prevent awkward moments by other guests who might have hesitated to join Stryker in a closed space. "Eighth floor, sir," the operator announced when the rising room came to a stop. He opened the gate and Stryker stepped out onto the emerald green carpet. The flooring was as thick as meadow grass under his boots but without the fresh outdoor smell. Stryker covered the hallway's meadow in long strides and stopped at the last door on the right. After one solid rap on the white, gold-trimmed door, it swung open.

"Come in, Mister Stryker." The hotel attaché opened the door, greeting him with a stilted smile. "Senator Hearst is in the bedroom.

He'll be out in a moment." He closed the door behind Stryker and asked, "Would you like any kind of refreshment, sir?"

Stryker eyed the tray on an engraved drum table by the widow. The bottle of Cognac with two crystal glasses did look inviting. "Cold water," he said instead. The attaché spun and left the room without further comment. Stryker had been in the senator's suite many times; nevertheless, he took a moment to stand and survey the furnishings. Plush forest green carpeting met walls painted green to match. All were trimmed with dark mahogany baseboards, crown molding, and door frames. In the center of the room, eight leather chairs, three on each side, one at each end, sat around a mahogany conference table, featuring an inlaid glass redwood in the center. A couple of leather wingback chairs sat by the drum table facing the bay window. The settee by the opposite wall was also leather. A man's room to be sure. At least the living room was, Stryker hadn't seen the bedroom. A toilet flushed beyond.

"Stryker!" Hearst hailed, coming from the bedroom. The senator was a tall man, not as tall as Stryker, maybe three inches shorter, but he stood rail thin and looked taller than his six feet. He was a coarse self-made man who dug out a fortune in the Comstock, and he sported a full beard, speckled gray in color, making his intense glare stand out all the more. He and Stryker got along well. "Thanks for coming so soon. Let's have a seat." He pointed toward the wingbacks. He offered no handshake; he knew better than to attempt a handshake with the mixed breed.

"Beautiful bay," Hearst said, nodding at the panoramic view beyond the bay window. "Someday they'll build taller buildings, and I won't be able to see it. Don't matter, I guess. I'll be dead by then."

"What's the job?" Stryker said.

"It's for a friend of mine, a business partner. He'll be here in a little while." Hearst re-positioned himself in the chair to face Stryker. Even though he'd met with Stryker several times, it was obvious the man still made him uneasy. The senator had heard stories.

"Before he gets here, I want to thank you for your help with Tami in Tahoe. I understand you were injured." He was currying favor. A United States senator curried favor with a killer. "Morgan told me Tami had a brand-new tavern built for her—and by the man who'd burned her out. That right?"

"Yes."

"Have much trouble with him?"

"No." In fact, Stryker did have a few difficulties. He killed three men to help with the persuading, and in an unrelated incident, where Stryker was partly to blame, an innocent girl was killed. Stryker also left out the reason the man who burned down Tami's taverns did so because he loved her. He knew Hearst still had affections for the woman, and he let the old man think he was solely responsible for Tami's new tavern.

"I added ten thousand to your bank account," Hearst said with a hint of a smile.

Stryker acknowledged the payment with a nod, and again asked, "What's the job?"

"John Mackay is a good friend and business partner. He is a self-made man like me. He got rich, extremely rich, after working years in the mines. He's an honest man, pays a fair wage, never cheated or welched on a deal, and never broke his word, but now he has a touchy problem. His wife, while living in Paris, had taken possession of an artist's painting. She—"

A knock on the door interrupted the senator.

The door opened. Apparently, Stryker figured, staff had been instructed to not make the senator come to the door. He hadn't noticed that with earlier visits. Hearst did seem a bit older to him now. The attaché entered with a tray holding a crystal water pitcher and two glasses. The glassware had *Ps* etched on them. "Your water, sir." He placed the pitcher and glasses on the drum table next to the Cognac. Tucking the tray under his arm, he filled the glasses and turned to leave. "Ah, Mister Mackay, sir."

Stryker turned and saw a man standing at the door. Unlike the staff member, the fellow waited to be invited inside.

"John!" Hearst roared, pushing himself to his feet. "Come in. I was just starting to tell Stryker about you." He scurried across the floor as fast as his rickety old legs could carry him, and the two men shook hands.

John Mackay wore an immaculately tailored, brown-striped suit, and it fit him well, but he appeared woefully awkward in it. Fancy threads could not refine the man. He was a stout five feet, ten inches, with a rugged face, a bushy mustache, and sad eyes. His rough hands poked out beneath his cuffs and looked permanently bent and curiously empty. You could easily imagine they were made that way after years of being wrapped around a pick handle–and they were.

John Mackay was one of the four *Bonanza Kings* with James Fair, James Flood, and William O'Brien. In 1873, they discovered the largest ore body of silver ever discovered in North America. Mackay led the digging in a section of Virginia City where other miners supposed it unproductive. The bonanza produced $181 billion in today's dollars. Mackay's portion was $50 billion. It took him twenty-one years of back-breaking digging in hard rock to finally hit it big.

"John, this is Mister Stryker," Hearst said, extending his hand toward Stryker. "He's the man I told you about. He may be able to help us with our problem." It wasn't a problem for the senator of course; however, it was apparent he wanted to connect the issue to himself before discussing the matter with Stryker. After all, he had paid the man a huge amount of money. That would probably play some part in convincing him to take on the job for his friend.

Stryker stood but did not approach the two men.

"Why don't we sit here at the table," Hearst said pointing at the conference table. "Kurtz," he said to the attaché. "Please bring what Mister Mackay would like to drink."

"Coffee's fine," Mackay said to the attaché, who nodded and spun smartly on his heels. Stryker suspected he might have been in the military.

To the visible relief of Hearst, Stryker pulled out a chair and sat at the table. His taking a seat most likely prevented awkwardness if Mackay had offered a handshake. Hearst and Mackay joined Stryker at the table. Hearst took the end chair. Mackay sat across from Stryker, leaning forward with his hands clasped together on the table.

"Mister Stryker, my wife, Marie, lived in Paris for a bit, and while there she bought a painting. The painting was stolen from her in Denver." Mackay got right to it. He was a no-bull-shit man.

Stryker said nothing. There had to be more to the story.

"She bought it from a girl named Gaby[1], a young woman in her late teens, Marie told me. We don't know how the artwork came into Gaby's possession. It was either given to her by the artist or she stole it from him, a Dutchman by the name of Vincent van Gogh. Gaby may have been a prostitute, after all, she did work in the brothel, but she also worked as a waitress in a restaurant cleaning tables. She could have cleaned rooms in the brothel too. Doesn't matter, I guess. The painting is of the place where van Gogh lived with another artist in the south of France, a man by the name of Paul Gauguin. It's called *The Yellow House*[2] (earlier called *The Street*.) Van Gogh may have actually given it to the girl, we don't know. He did give her his ear he cut off after an argument with Gauguin. Apparently, van Gogh is a gifted artist, but it seems at times he is quite mad.

"Now here is the problem. Van Gogh's brother, Theo, wants the painting returned to the van Gogh family. Marie may have bought stolen property, and there are rumors that it *was* stolen. The rumors were probably circulated by the jealous French. Marie does flaunt our wealth. Regardless of how she came to own the painting, I need to get it back and clear my name."

"John is known here, Stryker, as a man with impeccable honesty," Hearst added. "If news got out in San Francisco that his family dealt with stolen property, his reputation here would be ruined. You see, John owns the largest chunk in the Nevada Bank of San Francisco."

"Think you can help with this, Stryker? If so, name your price. I'll pay it." Mackay leaned back, slapping his palms on the table. "There, you have it."

Suddenly a strong gust of wind rattled the bay window. Then another blast hit it, followed by heavy sheets of rain that struck the panes with such force it threatened to break the glass. It was late in the afternoon, but not late enough for it to be as dark as it was outside. The storm had launched suddenly without warning. Seemingly angry it couldn't break the window the storm pounded the glass with hard-driving rain.

Mackay swung away from Stryker to watch the rain pelt the window.

Hearst swiveled around too. "Haven't seen a storm like that in a while," Hearst said, half rising from his chair.

Stryker rose, walked to the window, and stood watching the rain.

"Is he thinking about it?" Mackay whispered to Hearst.

"I don't know," Hearst whispered in reply, spreading out his hands. "Let's talk about something else while we wait." Louder he said, "Tell me about the cable, John."

After a brief pause, Mackay replied, "Oh, you mean the trans-Atlantic cable? There's more than one. You're talking about The Commercial Cable Company I own with Jim Bennett. We've laid two, and we're now planning a third."

Mackay and Hearst continued with their cable conversation, purportedly to give Stryker time to decide whether or not to take the job.

Stryker had already decided. He didn't think about the job while he stood by the window. He thought about how good it was to be out of the rain. He'd been out in downpours that soaked him to the bone, cold and miserable. He had often been caught in storms like it during the War. The Civil War…

In his mid-teens, Stryker was a crewman on a Parrott Rifle, a two-wheeled ten-pound cannon. He recalled a late afternoon that had rained hard. It was dark as night though, and in the air, bullets outnumbered raindrops. It had sure seemed that way. Blood and rainwater ran in rivulets over the ground. There were many cries for help and a lot of just plain crying. He couldn't see the men or boys, but he could sure hear 'em, even above the rain.

Sergeant Dempsey got it that day; he got one in the belly. Another tore away his lower jaw. Sarge lay in the mud, up on one elbow, trying to shout orders. Blood gushed out what remained of his mouth. After a while, he realized it was no good, and he motioned for the lieutenant to shoot him. The lieutenant put a pistol to his head and shot him. Shot him between the eyes.

Stryker turned away from the window and the rain. "I'll get your painting."

Hearst and Mackay abruptly interrupted their talk. They glanced at one another and then faced Stryker. "Good," they both said at the same time.

"What do you want for it?" Mackay asked.

"What it's worth to you," Stryker said, walking back to the table. "When and where was the last your wife saw the painting?" Stryker took a seat again.

"Marie was staying at the Windsor Hotel in Denver. On her way back from Paris, she stopped for a few days to see friends. Said she had left the painting in her room and went to see a performance at the Tabor Opera House, a couple of blocks away. When she returned, the painting was gone. Whoever stole it took jewelry as well."

"She reported the theft to the hotel or police," Stryker asked in a statement. He had an irritating habit of asking questions as a statement.

"I suppose so. When I asked her about it, she just said 'They don't know anything.' We communicate by telegraph. That's the last one I got from her, and I got it this morning."

"She's still in Denver," Stryker said.

"Yes."

"Tell her to stay there. I want to talk to her." With that, Stryker pushed back his chair, got up, and left.

"Is he coming back?" Mackay asked Hearst.

"Not today. But when he does, he'll most likely have the painting. Want some dinner?" Hearst asked.

Stryker had eaten stew the night before, but hot soup would warm a body on this cold rainy night. He didn't fancy running into Hearst and Mackay in the Grill Room. Soup and a steak were worth getting wet again. Running out on Morgan wasn't sitting well with him, and having to make conversation when in a foul mood could make him nasty. Stryker's almost always nasty, but sometimes he can be even nastier. Regardless, he wanted a damn steak. The Tadich Grill was on California Street, rainy blocks away. He'd settle for Rosie's on Mission Street. She cooked a good steak too.

He left the Palace out a side door leading to an alley, taking the most direct route to Rosie's. The hotel and other buildings through the alley sheltered him from the swirling wind, but the rain still fell heavily, pounding loudly on wooden crates stacked by the doors. Walking by a brick two-story building, he tightened his collar under the Stetson and tried not to step in puddles along the way. Stryker had traveled about halfway down the alley when he felt a poke in the middle of his back.

The "stop" and the hesitant "raise your hands," sounded as if the male giving the orders was a little unsure of himself. "I've got a gun," he added.

It felt like a gun barrel poked Stryker's back. He stopped and raised his arms.

"Give me your–" The mugger didn't finish because Stryker whirled, whipping his right arm against the hand which held the gun, knocking it out of the way. After that fraction of a second, a fired bullet snagged the outer edge of his coat. Stryker grabbed the man's wrist with his left hand and gripped the gun barrel with his right. Jerking upward, Stryker ripped the gun out of the assailant's hand. Holding the gun by its barrel, he swung the gun up and back before reversing its arc, and in a powerful blow, he smashed the gun butt against the man's temple. That movement was completed in what remained of a very brief second.

The mugger staggered sideways to the brick wall and crumbled to the ground. Stryker switched the gun to his left hand and pulled the sai. He knelt, grabbed a handful of the man's hair, and slammed his head against the bricks. The dazed man looked to be in his mid-twenties and reeked of booze. Shabbily dressed, he also needed to have a stern talk with his tailor. The fight in him was gone, and he just sat there in the rain and moaned. Stryker positioned the center prong at the man's left eye.

Bracing his shoulder against his hand, he lurched forward, driving the steel point into the man's brain. Stryker jiggled the sai and the moaning stopped.

Stryker wiped the sai on the man's ragged clothing and got to his feet. He dropped the gun between the dead man's legs, replaced the sai in its pouch, and tightened his collar tight around his neck. He then continued down the alley to Rosie's. No one got a second chance.

Stryker knew the dead man's history. Like others, he'd started out early ruining his life by drinking at a young age. The alcohol made him feel funny the first time, light-headed, and carefree. It was fun. He probably drank with his buddies. They had fun drinking together. Some of his drinking buddies realized booze wasn't good for them and they moved on, but not him. His buddies who left were missing out on the fun, he said. Oh, he got a job or jobs. As the drinking became more serious, he couldn't hold a job, and he changed jobs often. He needed the money to buy drinks, though. He began bumming money from friends when out of work. Eventually, the times between jobs grew longer and his friends grew fewer. He may have even tried opium by then. That made him feel even better, but opium cost money too.

When the jobs and the borrowing ran out, he turned to begging. It was degrading, but damn, he was thirsty. He drank or used opium to escape the life he lived. However, begging was hard work. Sometimes he'd have to stand and beg for hours before he got enough money to buy a drink. Opium became too expensive on his meager begging money. He made up pitiful signs to hold while begging, saying he was down on his luck, he'd lost his job, or he had a wife and kids. And the booze he bought was cheap rotgut. It didn't matter as long as it had alcohol. At twenty-five, he looked and smelled like shit, and people veered away from him. Then it took too long to get the money, so he stole a gun. He'd use it to get drinking money. It was stealing but the people he'd steal from could get more. He couldn't. Wasn't fair. Besides, it'd only take a few minutes to get money with a gun. He should have thought of a gun before. Maybe he wouldn't be where he is now. But tonight, he wanted a drink. His belly ached. He crawled out of the box crates he'd called home with a gun. His first victim would be the man coming down the alley on a cold rainy night. That man was Stryker.

Rosie's was packed. A coal stove in a corner heated the room, heated it too well tonight. Cigar smoke and steam from wet clothing hung heavily in the air. A large framed picture of Rosie and her staff hung on the rear wall. Kerosene lamps on bracket shelves lit up the room. The place wasn't very big, maybe eight or nine tables with red tablecloths on them. All the tables were taken. *Shit.* However, one table in the far corner only had one person at it. The man appeared to be in his mid-thirties. When he saw Stryker searching the room for a seat, he motioned an invitation to join him. He sipped a glass of red wine as he apparently waited on a meal.

Stryker hung his wet coat on the crowded coat rack and made his way across the room.

"You look familiar, thought that when you came in," the fellow said after Stryker sat. He wore horn-rimmed glasses and had the bookish look of a learned man. A fit man, he could have been an athlete in the not-too-distant past. He also sported a beard that ran along his jawline up to a full mustache, leaving space under his lower lip and around the chin bare. His greeting was friendly and his smile seemed genuine.

"Can't say the same," Stryker replied. He began to think he'd made a mistake coming to the table.

"Your eyes, sir. Not easy to forget."

Stryker studied the face across from him more intently but said nothing.

"I know this is a WAG, but were you ever at West Point after the War?"

Stryker knew two things. The reference to a WAG was military jargon for wild-ass-guess and the West Point inquiry probably meant the man had been at the Army's academy.

"Yes."

"I knew it!" He exclaimed. "You were my cadet platoon leader! Stryker, that's your name, right?"

Stryker relaxed a little, guessing now that he hadn't killed a relative of the man. "Yes, could've been. I was acting platoon leader over under-classmen my last year."

"I'll bet you made me do a thousand push-ups," he said with a laugh. "Join the Army and see the world, one inch to twenty-four inches above it." He smiled, crinkling the skin around his eyes. "What are you doing now Stryker?" The question didn't come off as sarcastic. The man wore a tailored suit. Stryker was somewhat underdressed, although the .44 on his hip was a nice accessory. The fellow could have been snide, but he wasn't.

"I take on jobs from time to time. And you?"

"At the moment, I'm President of the University of California and the director of the Lick Observatory. Don't know how long that will last," he finished with a scowl. "Name's Ed Holden, by the way."

"Holden, can't say I remember. It was a—"

"Care to order a drink, sir?" The twenty-something, shapely waitress, asked. She had dark hair, dark eyes, red lipstick, and a face that was a little too round, but she did a good job filling out her uniform. She came over to their table and interrupted them. Rosie probably urged quick table turns.

"Beer and a steak, medium well," Stryker said cryptically. The wait-ress left without repeating the order. Turning back to Holden, Stryker continued, "… long time ago."

"Indeed, and I've embarked on a path for which I may not be entirely suited. On top of that, my wife, Mary, has refused to be with me in Cali-fornia. She and the children live with her mother in St. Louis. I'm afraid my military training in the Army does not carry wide currency with petu-lant academicians and astronomers. Never knew men could be so damned petty."

"I've taken a trail not planned, myself," Stryker said. "Your positions sound impressive, Holden."

"I remember you tried to kill a boy, Stryker."

"I'm getting better at it."

Holden chewed on that a bit. Figured Stryker wasn't joking and changed the subject. "There's dissension at the observatory. I'm not a particularly good astronomer. I can write a research paper well enough, but I don't have the patience to stare through a telescope for hours at a time, even if it's the best in the world." Holden paused for comment from Stryker. Didn't get it. "Do you know what a seismograph is?"

"Yes, but never saw one," Stryker said.

"We started using one at the observatory to keep our telescopes accurately aligned–we have two telescopes up there. I actually had more interest in seismography than astronomy. We've set up eight seismographs in the California system around the Bay. I recently published a catalog on Pacific Coast Earthquakes." Holden leaned over the table and spoke in a hushed tone. "Stryker, I think San Francisco is due for a catastrophic earthquake sometime soon[3]." He sat back and continued. "And no one believes me."

Stryker thought of Morgan. "You're sure?"

"No doubt." Holden saw the waitress approaching with the food. "Here comes our dinners."

"Any idea how long?"

"You mean how long before one hits?" Holden asked.

The waitress placed the plates down in front of both men.

"Yes." Stryker cut into his steak. He waited for an answer before he bit into it.

"Could be next week. Could be ten years or more. Hard to say. But it's coming." Holden cut off a piece of chicken and plopped it in his mouth. "But Stryker…" Holden finished chewing and swallowed. "What really bothers me is this small but vocal group on the campus at Berkley." He laid his fork down on the table and wiped his mouth.

Stryker thought it would be a good time to pause with food and take a sip of beer. He had a feeling Holden had some serious shit to unload.

"They've been reading tripe by a foreign writer espousing a new world order for the masses." Holden drew a long-exasperated breath. "I tell you, I don't know how these kids find that nonsense to read. It's not well-published. I had to get a pamphlet from one of the students. Talks about all being under a socialist system where everyone got paid the same. Some German man by the name of Karl Marx wrote it. I personally don't see how that could possibly work. Would take productive levels to the lowest common denominator, not everyone works at the same level, you know. Regardless, if the young want to debate the merits of socialism among themselves, that's all right, maybe even a good thing, because it could engender thoughtful discussion. However, the students got in front of a major benefactor with shouts and hateful signs when she came on campus, and they frightened her away. Now she won't accept my person when I call on her."

Holden angrily stabbed the chicken with his fork. It stuck on the meat. He grabbed the protruding chicken bone and wrenched out the fork. He slapped the utensil on the table and tore off a piece of chicken with his teeth. He was clearly annoyed.

"Who's your benefactor?" Stryker asked, cutting into his steak with less anger than the professor.

"Phoebe Hearst, the senator's wife. And he's rich, dammit!"

"Senator George Hearst," Stryker said.

"Yes, you know him, do you?"

"Heard of him."

"I understand he can be quite cantankerous, and if he's turned on the school because of those kids… I was planning on that money for the new science building. I should just go back to West Point and teach."

"You know anything about art?" Stryker asked.

"You mean paintings and such?"

"Yes." Stryker cut into the steak again.

"Very little, actually. Why do you ask?" Holden picked up his knife and fork.

"A painting was stolen. Need information on it."

"Who's the artist?"

"Vincent van Gogh, a Dutch painter. Lives in France."

"I have heard of him!" Exclaimed Holden. "Read about him in the *Examiner*. Kind of deranged, I think. Don't know about his artwork, but I read he cut off his own ear," Holden chuckled, resting his forearms on the tablecloth, fork in one hand, knife in the other. Maybe the chicken wasn't all that good. "It did mention he'd only sold one painting, so it doesn't sound as if he's very good." Holden had another go with the chicken using the utensils.

"Two things, Holden," Stryker began. "Get me information about art collectors in Denver, then send what you find to me, care of the best hotel in Denver–you said you were good at research. Second, throw those damn kids out of your school or I'll kill 'em when I return. You do those two things, and I'll get your endowment for you."

Holden's forked meat hung suspended by his open mouth. "Who the hell are you?" He returned the chicken to the plate and leaned across the table. "Pardon my language, but what kind of work do you do?"

"Leaving for Denver in the morning." Having finished with his steak, Stryker scooted away from the table, got to his feet, and threw down a couple of dollar coins. "Good running into you again," he said, and he walked out of Rosie's.

Stryker stopped in a used bookstore around the corner and spent thirty minutes searching for a book on art. He finally found one. It wasn't very thick, and it had black-and-white pictures on some of the pages. He bought it for fifty cents and stuck it down the back of his pants with the top half still showing above his belt. He stood inside the shop for a few more minutes and waited for the rain to let up.

CHAPTER FOUR

Stryker hailed a horse cab back to the hotel. One might suspect the mixed breed chose not to take the alley because of the dead man. He hadn't thought of that. He was thinking about John Mackay and if he was worth the effort. After a while, he thought about Morgan and how good she felt under him. The only person to think about the dead man was probably the fellow who had to clean up the mess.

The cab got in line outside the arched entryway to the Palace. Cabs were lined up for half a block, waiting to enter the Grand Court where passengers could disembark out of the rain. Stryker grew impatient. He paid the driver and climbed out of the cab. He ignored the rain and walked into the hotel. Drenched and chilled, a hot mug of coffee with a shot of brandy called to him, and he headed to the bar. The bar with its lavish, ornate fixtures was without equal in the world, and the room was crowded with men drinking heavily and talking loudly. No wood on this bar. It had a chest-high green marble base with brass figurines blowing horns on the corners. Like all saloons in the day, it had a brass foot rail that ran the width of the bar. The countertop was adorned with thick, inlaid glass. It was the newest and finest, and only the best of refreshments were served there.

The drinkers and talkers took in the measure of the man with a .44

and made room for him. Stryker got his brandied coffee and moved away from the bar, allowing other thirsty men to step up and order their libations. He wove between the men and left the bar before he tried the coffee. It was good, hot, and rich, and the brandy added a sweet winery taste. He took another sip. That's when he heard the faint singing of a female. It sounded light and airy as if it floated to him on a breeze. It came from the Rose Room located just off the Grand Court. Her singing was melancholy, and Stryker, carrying the coffee, strolled across the plaza to the open double doors of the Rose Room. He stepped inside.

The songstress had a trim figure, and she wore a simple short-sleeve, light blue dress. A silver clip swept back one side of her blonde hair. The ends of which brushed against her shoulders. Even from across the expansive room, Stryker could see her eyes were light blue. She stood erect with her arms hanging at her sides. Her voice was delicate and clear, and she sang without the excessive flourish of voice or body movement.

Stryker was about to take another sip of the brew when he froze. He stared at the figure on stage, holding the mug in mid-air. A shudder pulsed through him. *Good God! Leigh? It can't be; I saw her die. A twin?*

Had she lived, his wife would have been a few years younger than Stryker today. His memory of her may have faded just enough to where the singer closely resembled what Leigh would have looked like if she were still alive. He had to remind himself Leigh was dead and she had no sister. He knew that. He would not approach the girl now, or later. That would be foolish. She has her own life, maybe a beau or husband. He'd have no right to interfere.

Stryker was about to turn and walk away when the girl saw him, and she stopped singing. She gathered herself and went on, but clearly, seeing Stryker had an effect. Nevertheless, he turned and walked out of the Rose Room. He had no right. His fierce countenance probably startled the girl.

He took the rising room to the seventh floor and strolled down the hall to his room still thinking about the girl. Upon opening the door, he was greeted by kerosene lanterns already lit and the bed was turned down. Nice touch by the hotel staff. The room was the same one Hearst reserved for him on other visits. It housed a king-sized bed, a separate bathroom with a tub, a mahogany desk with a chair, and two wing-back chairs by the window. The carpet was forest green and dark wood paneling lined the walls. Pictures of the sea and harbor hung on the paneling. He liked the room. It was a man's room. *Thoughtful of Hearst.* He threw his coat on the desk chair, laid the gun belt on the desktop, and sat on the bed to finish the coffee.

He couldn't help but think about what might have been. What might have been had Leigh lived? She missed out on so many years. *Damn.* He took a heavy breath. *Ah… damn.*

When he finished his coffee, he got up, went to the bathroom, and drew bath water. He undressed and climbed into the tub. After soaping his body, he leaned back and thought about the singer. He couldn't help it. Didn't matter. He was in his room, in the bath, and tomorrow he would get up and catch the train to Denver. She would be a memory, just like Leigh. The memory of the girl would slip further back in his mind, and he'd only recall his dead wife. *Good,* he thought, *enough of this.* He dunked his head in the water and sat up, preparing to lift out. *Too bad Morgan's not here. But she's probably still in Saratoga.*

Suddenly, there was a knock on the door.

Stryker got out of the tub and hurriedly toweled off. He grabbed one of the two white terrycloth robes hanging in the bathroom and threw it on. It made him look silly because the robes were always too short. The knock came again before he turned the doorknob.

"I was just thinking about you," Stryker said, opening the door.

But it wasn't Morgan. It was the singer from the Rose Room.

"May I come in?"

Stryker swung the door wider. She walked past him and stopped in the middle of the room. Eying him in the robe with his hair dripping wet, she said, "Sorry, I interrupted you."

"Want a chair?"

"Is it okay if I just sit on the bed?"

Stryker gestured an open palm toward the bed and drew up the desk chair for himself. He spun the chair around to face the bed as she sat. He scooted it a little closer but not too close. He felt awkward in the damn robe and made sure he kept his privates covered when he sat.

"My name's Mia," she began, crossing her ankles. "This is a good room," she said, looking around. Turning to address Stryker, she added, "It fits you. Tell me your name."

"Stryker. Neville's the first name." He tried hard not to stammer, but he figured his surprise upon seeing her was still noticeable.

"Downstairs, from across the room, you looked like my husband who died several years ago. The likeness startled me."

Her eyes were even bluer up close. "Too bad about your husband."

"I had to be sure you weren't him. I was told he'd been killed. They wouldn't let me see his body. He didn't have your eyes, though," Mia said, studying Stryker's face. "Are you married, Neville?" She glanced at his left hand.

"I… no. I'm not married."

"Why did you hesitate? *Were* you married?"

The girl asks a lot of questions. "Yes."

"What happened to her?"

"Killed in an accident years ago."

"Was she pretty?"

"She looked like you." *She looked exactly like you. And yes, she was beautiful.*

Mia smiled weakly. "I thought there was something when I saw you staring at me tonight. Sad coincidence. I mean, both of us thinking of how we reminded… you know." She didn't finish.

"Yeah." He couldn't think of anything to add either.

"It's really raining tonight." Mia slipped from the bed and went to the bay window. She stood there watching the rain hit the glass.

Stryker rose from the chair and stood beside her. He still hadn't managed to mine any suitable words.

"I had hoped you would have said Clayton," Mia said in a monotone, staring at the rain.

"Your husband's name."

"Yes." The rain pelted harder against the window now. "What was your wife's name, Neville?"

"Leigh," Stryker said. Lightening flashed in the distance. Far away and there was no thunder.

"You miss her?"

"Yes."

"I miss Clayton, too. I'd give anything to have one more day, just one more day with him. To feel his arms around me again.

"Even just an hour with her," Stryker said.

"Neville, you ever think of what might have been?"

"Try not to."

"What if we pretend? You and me." Mia turned to Stryker.

"No good, Mia."

"For one night, let's make-believe." Her voice rose. "We give each other one special night. You hold me. I pretend. You pretend. Nothing more. Just hold me. In the morning, we say goodbye and never see each other again."

Surprised at her suggestion, Stryker turned to Mia. Her blue eyes teared, searching for his answer. He paused for a moment, and then said, "There's another robe in the bathroom."

After turning down the lanterns, they got into bed and lay on top of the blankets. Mia curled up next to Stryker and he put his arm around her. Holding her close, he stroked her hair. She put her arm across him. His robe had parted slightly, and she laid her cheek against his chest. Her soft breathing tickled the hairs. She whispered something. Stryker couldn't hear what she said, but he squeezed tighter, and her tears moistened his skin. Neither spoke. They lay together, lost in their own thoughts, and in the wee hours of the morning they fell asleep.

The next day, Stryker rose first. It was getting light. He dressed and then leaned down to kiss Mia on the forehead.

Her eyes fluttered open. "Goodbye, Neville."

"Goodbye, Mia." He pivoted and opened the door. He hesitated for the briefest of moments before closing it behind him.

Stryker waited outside the door for a full half minute before he drew a deep breath and headed down the hall. It wouldn't have worked. Even if she'd wanted more, and him too. They'd be living a lie. He couldn't do that, and he suspected Mia felt the same. Nevertheless, it was a good night. It was a very good night.

The rain stopped early in the morning, but the streets remained wet and the cobblestones glistened. He'd left the hotel without stopping at the front desk. On an earlier trip to San Francisco, he learned Hearst kept a room open for him. The only thing he had to do was pick up the key when he checked in and leave it in the room when he wasn't coming back. Privileges and money provided privileges, and the senator had plenty of it. Riding on the cable car, he thought about his time with Mia. Then he thought about Leigh and decided he'd spent the night with Leigh.

Ahead, the Ferry House came into view with names of major cities like St. Louis, Los Angeles, Chicago, and New York painted above the arched entryways. The cable car stopped halfway around the turnabout and Stryker hopped off. He hailed a stableman and called for the roan. Figuring he'd need a horse in Colorado, he arranged for its passage with him to Denver.

The Ferry House was already crowded with passengers either waiting for the Oakland ferry or the train, and it was running a half-hour late. The place was a chaotic maelstrom of activity. Five different routes of cable cars came and went from the station. Eight boat slips along the docks dumped and received passengers. When the Southern Pacific pulled in, its locomotives rattled the entire building. Shouting vendors hawked their wares. The smell of freshly brewed coffee enticed Stryker to line up behind a group of rowdy young males from Cal-Berkeley University, at least that was the name embroidered on their sweaters. They were having a good time. It was Saturday morning and Stryker overheard the boy's conversations; the lads were waiting for the Oakland ferry. They were jabbering about an upcoming game called football with the Reliance Athletic Club. Interspersed were bits of talk about the San Francisco Stock and Bond Exchange. Far more attention was being paid to football than stocks. Apparently, they'd spent Friday studying about the stock market and were ready to release their energy at the future game. The boys struck Stryker as a bit haughty when someone outside their group butted in to ask about stocks or the game. They reminded him of certain upperclassmen when he attended West Point. It was not a good memory.

The boys picked up whatever special brew they ordered and moved their huddle toward the ferry gate. Stryker got a mug of hot black coffee and strolled to the Southern Pacific's gate. The train pulled into the station, and the workers de-coupled the coach cars, allowing the engine to be reversed on the turntable. He walked farther onto the loading platform and watched the roan get loaded into the livestock car. Satisfied, he rejoined the other passengers gathered near gate four.

Looked to be a full ride, he thought, judging the number of passengers waiting to board. The gates rolled back, and Stryker headed toward the rear of the second coach, figuring that increased the chances of grabbing his customary seat. It worked. He took a seat with his back against the rear wall. The previous night's rain left the coach smelling musty and the bench wet. The window had been left open. He swept the beads of water off the bench with his hand, sat down, and watched the rest of the passengers board, filling in the rows front to rear. As usual, the last row of seats to be taken was by Stryker. He wasn't the friendliest-looking fellow on the train.

Two men were the final passengers to come down the aisle. One man led the other, who followed closely. The man in front wore a badge. When they sat on the bench opposite Stryker, he saw why the second man kept so near the lawman. He was handcuffed. The officer gripped the empty cuff in his hand. A lawman often held the other half of the Taylor handcuffs in his hand, allowing him to jerk on a cuffed man, sometimes breaking his wrist without injury to himself. Their bench wasn't as wet, but by the look on the lawman's face, he wouldn't have cared. A few passengers had seen the handcuffs as the two men walked past but said nothing. They must have figured it was none of their business. That is not to say the women failed to notice the handcuffed man. He was quite handsome with blond hair, blue eyes, trimmed stature, and he was reasonably well-dressed. Although the blue-striped suit looked as if it had been worn a few days. The marshal, not as handsome. He was a burly man and had bushy eyebrows, rugged features, and wore no suit. It was wool slacks, a white shirt, and a cowhide coat for him. He also held a revolver outside its holster, down his right side. They took a seat on the bench across from Stryker.

The marshal eyed Stryker in a way that suggested he was suspicious of the mixed breed. The lawman rested the pistol on his thigh, aimed at Stryker.

"I'm no threat, Marshal. Point that gun away from me," Stryker said.

The marshal sat the pistol by his side opposite the prisoner. "Bart here killed a man. Taking him back to hang in San Jose. My name's Rickert, Mitch Rickert, and I'm the marshal in San Jose." Rickert maintained a steady gaze on Stryker.

Stryker shifted his attention to the prisoner.

"The man killed my wife. I killed him," the young man stated matter-of-factly.

His story had a familiar ring to it.

"She weren't your wife, Bart," Rickert growled and spit on the floor.

"We got married the week before, mister," he spoke to Stryker. "And my name's Bartholomew. I don't like diminutives."

Stryker dipped his Stetson, accepting both declarations. He believed the prisoner's claim of marriage, and he wasn't particularly fond of diminutives either.

The lawman saw it and said, "Hell, she was a damned whore—she worked in a brothel."

Outside, the couplings clanged down the tracks in sequence and the cars lurched forward. Passengers facing rearward, swayed with it, including the marshal and Bartholomew. That broke the conversation. Stryker peered out the window and watched the houses of southern San Francisco roll past. He'd heard enough from the two men. He didn't blame the kid, and the marshal had a job to do.

Stryker had known several whores, prostitutes, and never thought of marrying one. There were a few he liked, though. The way he saw it, many a woman married a man for his money. And every time she bedded down with him, it was for the money. Different? Not the same? He figured those married women, at least, had similarities with the soiled doves in bordellos. The married ones were with only the one man. But if a woman in a whorehouse only fucked the same man over and over again, she'd still be called a prostitute. And girls in whorehouses were a lot less haughty than some snooty wives he'd known–a couple of them in the biblical sense.

These were Stryker's ruminations when he heard the punch. He knew the sound right away. It was the same as someone who had just hand-slapped a side of beef hanging in a butcher shop.

Stryker snapped his head around and saw the marshal recoil from the blow. Then Bartholomew hit him again. The kid was using his left hand and he drew back for another. Before he could deliver it, Rickert shot him. Shot him in the stomach.

"She was my wife, fucker," Bartholomew said, grimacing. He put his hand to his side, and when he pulled it away, it was covered with blood. He cocked his arm a third time.

Rickert fired again, and the kid took the bullet in his chest. Bartholomew slumped in the corner of the bench, dropped his chin, and with a soft moan, he closed his eyes and died.

The coach got quiet. Curious men half-rose off the benches and strained their necks to find out what caused the shooting. Men in the closest rows to the shooting ducked down and stayed down, pulling women down beside them. No one yelled out to ask what happened. Only the clacking of train wheels interrupted the silence.

Rickert dropped the handcuff and rose to his feet. He faced the curious onlookers, and said, "Sorry, folks. The prisoner tried to escape. I had to shoot him." Several women groaned. Rickert scowled at the lot of them and yelled, "He killed a man. Didn't want to give him a chance to kill again." He sat back down, muttering, "Stupid women."

The conductor entered the coach to collect tickets. A man in the second row pulled him aside and told him about the shooting. The conductor straightened and started toward the rear. He came down the aisle, never taking his eyes off Stryker, to the last row.

"He dead?" The conductor, a plump fellow in his fifties, lifted a meaty finger and pointed at Bartholomew. He then noticed the badge on Rickert. The marshal still held the gun in his hand. "You shot him?" He asked.

"He punched me, trying to escape. He ain't movin'." Rickert placed his hand on Bartholomew's neck. "Yeah, he's dead." Drawing back, he looked at the body a bit longer and said to the conductor. "You got someplace to put 'im til we get to San Jose?"

"Cattle car, I guess. I'll signal for the train to stop." The conductor swung about, walked briskly to the front, and disappeared out the door.

Passengers turned back around and resumed their low murmurings.

Rickert saw Stryker staring at him. "I don't think he was really trying to escape," the lawman admitted.

"No, reckon not," said Stryker.

"What the hell did he want with a whore for a wife?"

"Seeds of romance can germinate in unlikely places, I reckon."

Rickert chewed on that for a bit, and then said, "The boy he killed wanted another round with the girl. She was staying at the whorehouse while Bartholomew was gone for a week. Don't know where he went. Anyway, when the girl turned the boy down, he slapped her, and she fell, hitting the side of her head on a table edge. Killed her. Didn't prosecute him. Was a' accident. And another thing, that boy was the mayor's son. Besides, she was just a..." Rickert saw Stryker's menacing gaze and probably figured he'd used 'whore' enough. "When Bartholomew got back," Rickert nodded at the body, "he went crazy, found the other boy, and shot him."

"Shakespearian tragedy," Stryker deadpanned.

"Huh?"

The train slowed. Ahead of the coach, Stryker heard the engine brakes squeak and his body swayed forward. Someone in the front row asked, "Why are we stopping?"

The conductor came through the door and announced that the train would be making a ten-minute stop. He didn't say why. The passengers probably knew. He walked through the car and out the back to the car behind them. After a few minutes, he returned.

The conductor helped the marshal carry Bartholomew's body out the coach's rear door. Then later, Stryker watched the railman walking on the ground outside toward the engine. Shortly after that, the train started moving again. The marshal never showed back up, and Stryker figured he must have stayed in the cattle car with the body.

The landscape out Stryker's window now went from a smattering of houses to rolling hills with small stands of oak, willow, and bay laurel. The San Francisco Bay showed beyond the windows across the aisle for a mile or so and then passed out of sight. Then the ground flattened and stayed like that until the train rolled into San Jose.

In San Jose, Stryker stepped off the Southern Pacific and waited in the station for forty-five minutes. He grabbed a sausage biscuit and got coffee in the cup he brought from his saddle bag. Then he and the roan boarded the Central Pacific rail line for the two-day ride to Denver. He'd been to Denver before, but it had been a while. He was on his way west to San Francisco after his wife died. Going home. Why, he wasn't sure. His folks were dead and he had no friends there, nor anywhere else for that matter. Maybe he was destined to meet Morgan and Hearst. Didn't know. The senator gave substance to Stryker's life, a job to do every now and then. And the woman… well, she provided what a good woman can give a man.

The coach filled in except for the bench across from Stryker. He sat in the last row as usual. Roughly two-thirds of the seats were filled. Mostly men, some in suits, two pairs of women who looked like school teachers, and four or five middle-aged couples. Stryker didn't count them. He sat alone in the rear. He wasn't in the mood to talk about the weather, ranching, politics, or anything else. He had picked up the *San Francisco Examiner* in San Jose and read when he felt like it. He looked out the window, watched the grass-covered hills roll by, and sipped coffee, which was now only lukewarm. After nursing the brew down to half-full, he opened the Crowell bag holding the sausage biscuit. Folding the paper around its lower half, he bit into it and chewed slowly, enjoying the peppered sausage stuffed inside the hardtack. The biscuit itself was hard and crunchy, but the grease from the sausage softened the dough. Good stuff. After a couple more bites, he took another swill of coffee. It was half-past noon, and he'd finished eating, wishing he'd bought two biscuits instead of just one. He drank the last of the coffee and picked up the paper to read. A half-hour later, the paper settled in his lap. The steady monotony of the train's wheels clacking on the rails made him sleepy. A recollection, that could have been a dream, swirled around a real event in the past. It was a vivid little scene lasting several minutes.

At West Point, Stryker was one of two cadets who'd been in the Civil War prior to entering the Army's prestigious academy. Both men had seen battlefield action. The other man, John Bourke, had been awarded the Medal of Honor at the Battle of Stone's River, Tennessee. Whether it was jealousy, envy, or disdain against Stryker, cadets not in the war went out of their way to disassociate themselves from him. Their attitude toward Stryker developed immediately after rumors circulated in the dorm halls that Stryker spent two-and-half years with an artillery crew during the war. Those rumors also stated he'd not been awarded any citations. One might have thought Stryker would have been admired for fighting in the war, but that wasn't the case. He was just a regular enlisted man during the conflict and was now trying to become an officer. He had no medals, and he had no pedigree. The cadets resented him, and a few were even hostile.

Entrants into West Point had to be appointed, or recommended, by a politician at the federal level or a high-ranking Army officer. More than one officer who'd seen the carnage of battle didn't encourage their sons to join the military. Often, appointments were secured by those who were politically connected. Prestigious families, well-to-do families, and fathers with influence were eager to jump-start a son's career who'd acquired officer rank. The war was over, and with no discernable prospect of dangerous duty, a young man could spend a few years in uniform without risk of life or injury and gain status and repute.

Stryker secured an appointment to the academy without family connections. He got in based on a recommendation from General Crook.

Non-prior military cadets proudly wore medals given to them for marching or close-order-drill. Stryker's cadet uniform had no medals for marching. He didn't excel in close-order drill either.

A bad memory.

West Point held an annual run and shoot championship each year to determine the best marksman after running a full mile. Stryker, a sophomore, had come in second his freshman year and was favored to win since last year's winner graduated. The Academy had thirty-eight enrolled cadets.

The day of the race was a sunny day at almost noon. A band played for the cadets and staff, and the eighty-five townspeople had come to see the competition. Inside the barracks, four runners were warming up and doing stretching exercises. The single-story barracks was a long rectangular building. Individual metal-framed beds were positioned along the walls and were tightly made with wool blankets and blocked pillows. A wooden foot locker sat in front of each bunk. Pairs of brightly polished boots were aligned by and next to a shiny fifteen-inch brass shoehorn. The three cadets doing stretch exercises in the center bay wore shorts, cotton t-shirts, and lace-up canvas shoes, all paid for by one of the boy's fathers. Stryker, the fourth runner, wore military-issued pants and shirt, a pair of army-green wool socks, and no shoes. Five friends of the three cadets wearing running outfits gathered around them, offering advice and encouragement. Stryker stretched by himself in a corner.

One of the friends watched Stryker doing his warm-ups and said, "I got an idea." The cadets and runners huddled together and talked hurriedly in hushed tones, punctuated with an occasional outburst, "Yeah, yeah," followed by laughter. They broke the huddle and wearing big shit-eating grins encircled Stryker. The runners stood back, watching what was about to happen.

"You gonna win today, Stryker?" The cadet with the idea asked. He wasn't a large boy, but he looked tough enough. "Me and the boys here will be rootin' for you. Won't we fellas?"

"We sure will!" The other four cadets chimed in, laughing.

Stryker didn't answer, and he wasn't laughing. He knew they were up to something.

"Those runners over there," the tough-looking cadet said, hooking a thumb over his shoulder, "got running shoes on, but they don't stand a chance against those army socks you're wearing." The cadets burst out laughing again. The three runners, who'd stopped stretching, laughed too. "Yessir, they're real racing socks," the cadet doing the talking said. "Let me take a close look at 'em." He sidled closer to Stryker, turning sideways and bending at the knees. "They sure look fast!"

Suddenly, one of the cadets behind Stryker shoved him. It was a hard shove, and Stryker planted a foot forward to keep his balance. That's when one of the cadets stomped on Stryker's foot and broke two of his metatarsal bones. The crunch echoed around the bunkhouse.

Stryker powered forward off of his good foot, attacking the stomper. The cadet fell on his back between two of the beds. Stryker leapt on top. He grabbed a shoe horn off a foot locker and jammed it in the boy's mouth. He was about to drive it through his throat when hands from behind him pulled him off.

"Holy shit, Stryker! You gonna kill him?" One cadet yelled.

They had Stryker on his back, pinned to the floor. He lay there, glaring up at them.

The stomper was beside him, coughing and bleeding from his mouth.

One of the cadets helped the stomper up and took him to sick bay. The three runners fled the building, and the cadets holding Stryker down released him and sprinted outside too. Stryker hobbled after them but couldn't catch any of the boys.

He didn't race that day; another runner won, and the incident wasn't reported. Throughout the rest of Stryker's four years at West Point, the cadets left him alone. Stryker won the next two annual races.

Stryker woke with a start. The sound of clacking train wheels returned when he became fully awake. Normally, a part of his brain stayed alert to warn him of threats. It was a sixth sense he'd developed in the war and it stuck with him. His subconscious brain must have suspended the monotonous clacking, judging it to be no threat, and blocked it out. He even blocked out friendly artillery fire the night before a battle, and yet he would wake to a twig snap. The brain of a soldier sharpens and focuses differently when his life is on the line. This is one of the reasons a soldier is never the same after the military.

If a person were to ask a soldier, "What is the one thing you missed most while in the Army?" If he was truthful, he probably won't say his mother or his father, home cooking, friends, or even his girl. Instead, the response will often be, "A good night's sleep."

Outside the window, flat terrain gave way to rolling green hills as the train swung through the Mount Diablo gap. Upon shooting the gap, the land flattened out again approaching Stockton.

Stryker had made this trip several times for Hearst, although not all the way to Denver. He knew what to expect while peering out the window, flat farmland with scattered cottonwoods, box elders, and willow trees up to Sacramento, and then after that, the landscape would change to rising elevations and evergreen trees.

Two hours more and the train pulled into Stockton. The conductor came in and called out, "Fifteen-minute stop!" Several riders got off the coach and walked behind the station to the restrooms. Stryker followed but went to the cattle car to check on the roan. He took the water bucket and went outside to the water trough, filled it, and returned to the car. Then he pulled a handful of oats from the saddle bag and threw them on the floor. Satisfied with the horse's care, he went to the restroom and came back around to the station platform. New passengers had spilled out of the station, and they had joined those re-boarding. By the look of the crowd, Stryker expected the three cars to be full. Stryker hopped back on the rear coach, took his regular seat, and watched people out the window as they boarded.

A middle-aged couple caught his eye. The large square-set man who could have been Stryker's age accompanied his petite wife and their two teenage boys. The boys stood behind their parents and pretended to box with each other, annoying the other passengers. That is until one boy pushed his brother and he bounced off his father. The father turned, grinned, and cuffed his son upside his head. That ended the boxing. It was not a punishing blow, but hard enough to curtail the horseplay. Stryker sensed the father wanted his sons raised tough, but horseplay around other passengers was unaccepted. The boys laughed and pushed one another more gently, being careful not to bump their father again. When they boarded, the father pointed toward the rear of the car. He gave the boys a good-natured push. The man guided his wife to take a seat near the front. Stryker had seen fathers like him before. He often thought some men tried to make their sons something they themselves were not, and he wondered how many sons paid the ultimate price for their father's vicariousness. The lads came down the car and seated themselves on the bench seat facing Stryker. Upon seeing the steady gaze of the mixed breed watching them, they quieted down. Stryker turned and looked out the window. The sun was out. It had turned into a decent day.

A few minutes after everybody boarded, the couplings clanged and the train started moving. It was twenty minutes or so before one of the boys got up the nerve to talk to Stryker. They'd whispered back and forth, "You ask him."

"No, you ask him." They exchanged words several times before one of them got the nerve.

"Were you in the war, mister? Our father was."

Stryker nodded, dipping the Stetson.

"North or South?" The other boy asked. They scooted forward, eager to engage. They could have been twins, each with blond hair, green eyes, medium build, and freckles. They looked fifteen, maybe sixteen, but not more than that. They were fresh-faced, ready to live life, or… die trying.

Stryker didn't like these two. He didn't care much for their father either. He thought about not replying, but he looked out the window at the passing landscape, and said, "North." He sat back, stretched out his legs, crossed them, and pulled the Stetson down over his brow.

"So was our father," the boys said at the same time. "He was at Gettysburg. "His name's Rawlings, Roy Rawlings. Do you know him?"

There were over two million men in the Union Army. Of course, Stryker would not know the man. The Stetson stayed down.

Not giving up. "Were you in any big battles? We would've gone and fought, but we weren't born then." They shared a silent giggle.

Stryker ignored them. He never talked about the war. *Who the hell has good memories about the slaughter of 620,000 men?* And the North lost 100,000 more than the South.

"Kill any them Gray-Bellies?" The boys exchanged glances.

There was a long pause before Stryker raised the brim with a forefinger. Then, he said, "You two have names."

"I'm Noah. My brother's Ethan," Noah supplied. He sat directly across from Stryker.

"I'll tell you about a Rebel I killed in the Battle of Antietam." Stryker straightened and uncrossed his legs.

The boys nodded and scooted even closer to the edge of the bench. Ethan leaned forward and rested his elbows on his knees. Noah did too.

"We fought in a cornfield." Stryker looked out the window and drew a long breath. "It rained all night, and the fog hung heavy on the ground. We fought all morning. Each side going back and forth." He turned away from the window and faced the two boys eager to hear about the battle.

"I was about your age, I guess. They had me on a Parrott gun. You know what that is?"

Ethan and Noah shook their heads.

"It's an artillery gun. I was one of eight crewmen on it and the youngest. We started firing the gun before daylight. Miller's field was thirty acres of corn but with the fog, we couldn't see much. But by the end of the day, all the corn stalks were gone, cut down by bullets and shrapnel. It was the bloodiest single battle in American history; twenty-three thousand casualties."

The boys hung on every word.

"By noon, six of the gun crew, including the sergeant, were dead. The corporal and I got the gun loaded and ready to fire. The Rebels came through the corn, running and yelling, shooting as they ran. The corporal fired the gun, and it exploded, killing him. It blew me off my feet and knocked me out. When I came to, the regiment of riflemen and I were ordered to sweep through the corn rows, looking for wounded. Another soldier shoved a rifle at me. The captain told us to bring in Union wounded and kill the Rebels. He said the battlefield hospital was overwhelmed. We fixed bayonets and started out. Don't know if the captain was trying to save Union lives, or if he wanted payback for killing so many of us. We Yankees won the field. Confederates pulled out and left us to search for wounded."

Stryker drew a long breath and went on. "Fog and smoke from the gunfire still hung heavy in the air, and I got separated from the others. I was still dizzy. Men yelled for help; there was a lot of moaning and crying out there ahead of me. I couldn't see 'em in the fog, but I could hear them."

"Were you scared?" Noah asked.

"I was scared all day." Stryker's pale eyes narrowed, daring the boys to say something. They didn't. "I went down a corn row. There were lots of dead bodies, some alone, some clumped together. Ammunition pouches, mess kits, equipment, papers, letters, and lots of letters were scattered all over.

"About halfway down the cornrow, I found a wounded Rebel trying to crawl back to his lines. I guess that's where he was headed. His knee looked like shrapnel tore it apart. The bottom half of his leg was twisted around. Maybe his pant leg was all that held it together. There was a bloody trail behind him for twenty feet or more, with bloody pools marking where he'd rested. I put the gun barrel against the back of his head and pulled the trigger. It didn't fire. He rolled over, and I saw how young he was. He was my age or younger. I hadn't quite turned sixteen."

Noah and Ethan looked surprised.

"I lied about my age—needed the money. Anyway, me and the Rebel stared at each other for a while. His face was dirty and streaked under his eyes where he'd been crying."

"'My leg's hurt,' he told me. I could tell that. From what I could see, it'd been blown apart. I didn't say anything. 'You gonna help me?' he asked. I shook my head. He turned over to start crawling again, but I guess his strength was gone, and he just lay there not moving. Finally, with some effort, he rolled on his back, and he just lay there looking up at me. 'I can't make it,' the kid groaned to me."

By now, the silly enthusiasm had fallen off the faces of Noah and Ethan.

"'Can't you get somebody to help me?' he asked me. He'd gotten up on an elbow and was staring at the ground as he spoke. 'No,' I told him.

'What you gonna do?' His voice got higher like he was gonna start crying. 'I gotta kill you,' I said to 'em."

Stryker breathed in.

"'Why?' Then he turned his face up to me and fell back on his back. 'Why you gotta do that?' He looked pretty scared then. 'My captain told me to, too many wounded,' I told him."

Stryker then added, "I left out it was because he was a Rebel. 'No, please,' he said, begging me."

Ethan's mouth dropped open. Noah cleared his throat. Their eyes got wider.

"I pointed the bayonet at his belly. He started crying and raised his hands up to me. I shoved down on the blade. It didn't go in very deep, but it was in enough for him to feel it. He wrapped his hands around the bayonet and tried to push it out. I put my body weight into it and pushed harder. The blade sank deeper, cutting his hands. Then, I pulled it out and looked down on him."

"You killed him?" Noah asked incredulously.

"No, he didn't die right away. He began praying, telling God how sorry he was for some of the things he'd done. He kept saying over and over how sorry he was and asking for forgiveness. I stuck him again, and he screamed. I stuck him again, and he prayed louder. I must have stuck him four or five times before he stopped praying. I started to run then, figuring I'd killed him, but I heard him calling for his mama.

"I didn't go back. I kept on going down the cornrow. I came to more wounded, but I never stopped for 'em. I just kept on walking to the end of the cornfield. Another Union soldier was helping one of our own who'd been shot in the thigh. He asked me to get on the other side and help him, which I did, and we made our way back up the cornrow.

"We passed the Rebel boy. He was on his back with his eyes and mouth open. None of us said anything. I saw flies crawling around his eyes, and there was blood on his mouth with flies there too. I figured he was dead then."

Stryker paused, and said, "Yeah, I remember that day when I killed my first gray-belly up close. You boys want to hear about another?"

"We're gonna go up and see about our folks," Ethan said. "Come on,

Noah." They got up and walked toward the front of the coach. Ethan leaned down to his parents, said something, and they scooted over to make room for the boys to sit with them. The family got off the train in Sacramento.

Stryker watched them through the window. The boys trailed behind their parents. There was no horseplay now. He watched as they met another family on the platform with three other children, a boy, and two girls, who appeared to be the same age as Noah and Ethan. Their big smiles and laughter indicated that they were excited to see one another, except for Noah and Ethan that is. Then they all disappeared into the station. Stryker sat staring out the window at the wooden, red-painted, single-story building, wishing the story he'd told the boys hadn't been true.

"War is hell," Stryker finally told himself. He tried to put the memory of the Rebel boy behind him. Of course, he knew that wouldn't happen. He'd often tell himself the boy would have bled to death. Didn't help. It was a regret he put in the dark hold with the others, and no matter how crowded it got in that damn thing, there was always room for more. *I'll make more*, Stryker admitted. *And shove 'em in with the rest.* He turned away from the window and lowered the Stetson.

CHAPTER FIVE

Stryker stepped off the train. He asked and was told he had fifteen minutes; it was enough time to buy a cup of coffee and a paper. Something to drink, something to read. It took him ten minutes. He got back on the train and was reading the paper when passengers reboarded and new ones got on. After the talk with the boys, he kind of hoped someone interesting would get on the train and they could have a good conversation.

Someone did, and she was good-looking.

She and an older bespeckled man in a rumbled suit came down the coach aisle. The woman strode purposefully erect, carrying a black brief-case. Empty seats were available, but she guided them to the last seat across from the man reading the *Financial News,* a British daily newspaper. How anyone got hold of that newspaper in America may have piqued her interest. The woman and the man with her settled in the seat across from the reader. The date on the paper read June 10th, which made the edition six weeks old. She couldn't see the man behind the paper. The reader, of course, was Stryker.

The train had pulled out of the station a half hour earlier, and it took another twenty minutes before Stryker lowered the newspaper. It would have been difficult to say who was more surprised, Stryker or the woman. Stryker, because he didn't expect an attractive woman to appear out of nowhere. He hadn't seen her outside at the station, but then he'd been reading the paper. Or perhaps the woman, because she hardly expected such a vile-looking man to be reading the *Financial Times*.

Nevertheless, the woman was the first to speak. "You have an interest in financial matters?"

"I used to," Stryker replied, taking the moment to make a quick study of her features. Shortly cropped blonde hair, intelligent hazel eyes with radiating crows-feet, reasonably tan skin, slender. She was perhaps five feet seven inches, but it was hard to tell; she was sitting down. Her mouth was a little too wide with nice lips, and other than that he didn't judge her appearance too closely. Okay, of course, he did. After all, Stryker is a man. She wore a khaki belted skirt, a white blouse, and a short-waisted brown leather jacket. The lines on her face put her age around forty, a young forty perhaps, but at least forty.

"In the station, I heard two boys telling their parents about a man on the train, who'd told them a story about killing a boy in the war. They were quite shaken by it. I'll make a wild guess and say you're that man."

Stryker's failure to acknowledge one way or the other most likely told the woman she'd guessed correctly. He stared back and said nothing.

"I wasn't anywhere near that terrible conflict; however, I suppose the brutality of it makes a man do awful things," she said.

"Only to end evil."

"Yes," she said. The corner of her mouth twitched. Could have been the hint of a smile, or perhaps, remembering a painful experience.

It took a while for the woman to digest what Stryker said. Finally, she responded with, "My name's Dagan, Dagan Talbert." Dagan did not extend her hand.

"Neville Stryker."

"Tell me about yourself, Neville."

He didn't, not immediately anyway. *Why is she asking? Who's the man with her?*

Finally, Dagan said, "Your comment about evil piqued my interest. I'd like to hear what experience you had with it."

The train rocked along at twenty miles an hour. A good many of the passengers were chattering with one another at about the same speed. Some spoke with acquaintances. Some struck up conversations with strangers. It would be a while before they settled into idle boredom. Three men sat by themselves, idly staring ahead, and one elderly woman, who was also alone, had her face in a book. The two rows of bench seats beyond Dagan toward the front of the car were empty. In the third row, an elderly man and woman sat talking. They could have been a couple. Their discourse ran easy. Stryker could barely hear them. Across the aisle, three rows of rear seats were also vacant.

"Subjugation of man is evil, enslaved, or otherwise," Stryker said.

"What's otherwise?"

"A man's earnings confiscated against his will."

"Or forced to give up property. But go on. Tell me more." Dagan wiggled her hips to adjust her skirt.

"A while back, I came upon a mining town called Bickford. A gang of political types had ridden in earlier and convinced the townsfolk to share what the mine produced equally. They'd killed the mine owner and the mayor. They changed the name of the town to Egalitaria. The gang leader called himself The Sharehelper. He stole most of the money. The mine soon closed. Turned out, the miners wanted to keep what they made, or they wouldn't work."

"Then what happened? Did they all leave?" Dagan asked.

"No. The widowed owner got the mine back, and the men went back to work."

"This Sharehelper man, what about him?"

"I killed him."

Dagan, who had been inching forward, listening to Stryker, drew back.

Before she could think of something to say, Stryker added, "The widow hired me to kill him."

Dagan collected herself. "Interesting story. Do you often perform such duties?" She paused and then realized Stryker wouldn't answer. "Never mind," she said. Her expression brightened. "I should like to meet such a woman."

"Tell me about you," Stryker said. "Where you're going and what you'll do when you get there." Stryker rattled it off as an order rather than a simple request, aggravated for giving what he considered too much information about himself.

"All right, I will. My husband wasn't killed, though," Dagan said. She took a long breath and gathered her thoughts.

"My partner here, Rudolf, designed and built a new type of power system for a locomotive. He's German and shy. He prefers I do the talking. A mechanical genius, he did the inventing. His shop is in a rented warehouse in Augsburg, Germany. It took years of hard work and frustration, and he only managed to construct a small-scale prototype. It didn't use steam and wasn't fired by wood or coal. At first, he experimented with kerosene, like in lamps, but that didn't work. So he had to learn how to distill crude oil. He built his own boiling tanks, coils, and distillation towers. For two years, he tried different liquids, cooling them at various temperatures. He had to get the viscosity mixture just right for combustion. His engine wasn't fired by ignition. Instead, combustion occurred with extremely high compression. Once he was able to produce the appropriate fuel oil, he had to match the firing with cylinder pistons to power up a generator, he also had to develop and produce electricity to turn an electric motor. And yes, he built that too. The motor turned the wheels. He had no development manual. He created each phase of the power system as he went along. It took thirteen years. All this is what he told me. I may have some of it wrong. Now finally, he's ready to build a new, full-scale engine, but he's out of money. That's why Rudolf is here in the United States. He can't get backers in Europe. I'm trying to help him raise it. I have connections, or at least thought I did, in San Francisco. We were turned down. The would-be backers in San Francisco said the whole thing sounded like folly. I'm on my way to Virginia City. There are rich men there, so I'm told, who take risks."

"What do you get out of it?" Stryker figured she wouldn't help for free.

"Ten-percent ownership, if he's successful," Dagan quickly added.

"You didn't meet with the right men in San Francisco."

Dagan thought about what Stryker just told her, and then said, "I'll be frank. You now know the real reason we came to the back to sit with you. You can help us?"

"Not now." Stryker glanced at Rudolf who stared blankly at him, and then he added, "I have another job to do."

It is doubtful Rudolf traveled to the United States. However, he was able to raise enough money to develop his new engine. Rudolf had continuous problems with competitors and was hounded by the German government who insisted he give them the rights to his motor. On September 29, 1913, he boarded a ship for London to meet with a competitor for the purpose of resolving differences. He was on the *SS Dresden* steamer and during the trip, he jumped overboard and drowned himself. His body later washed up on shore. Before Rudolf set sail, he'd left a bag for his wife with a note telling her not to open it until the following week. Inside the bag were 20,000 German marks, worth US $120,000.

It's too bad he never knew what an enormous contribution he made to mankind. Today, there are millions of his engines in use around the world. Those engines are named after Rudolf, whose full name was Rudolf Christian Karl Diesel.

By the time Stryker and Dagan finished discussing Rudolf's motor and finances, the train began its climb into the Sierras. They continued sporadic discourse, but the topics were lightweight, talking about stuff people usually do when filling empty spaces. Stryker normally wouldn't carry on such vacant chatter, but it was one of the few times in his life he chose not to be rude. They discussed the weather and the Sierra's scenery. Dialogue dragged on slower than the Central Pacific crawling up the mountain. He was relieved when Dagan and Rudolf stepped off the train in the supply town of Colfax and didn't reboard. Stryker didn't know if Dagan and Rudolf had business in the town, or if they simply missed the train. He focused a somber gaze out the window and watched the Sierra Mountains pass by.

Huge granite boulders, shaped smooth and round by centuries of glacial grinding, peppered the cliffs, adding to the stunning beauty of mountains blanketed with towering evergreens. Ahead and above the curved tracks, snow still clung to the peaks, as though an artist had painted them to contrast the azure sky. But no artist could ever capture on canvas the scene Stryker saw out the window. It would be impossible to paint its true colors, much less get brilliant white clouds to float lazily in the sky above the mountains. All that disappeared as the train entered the first of fifteen tunnels. Near Donner Pass, the train passed through forty miles of snow sheds, blotting out some of the most beautiful views in the world. Stryker would have napped in the sheds and tunnels had it not been for the thunderous locomotive echoing off the walls and the thick black smoke.

After a two-hour stop-over at the Cardwell Hotel on the summit, the Central Pacific began rolling down the curved tracks of Sierra's eastern slopes[1]. After more tunnels and sheds during the downhill run and Donner Lake came into view. Smaller than Lake Tahoe and not as pretty, Donner Lake was nevertheless a sight to see. Shortly after passing the lake on a gentler grade, the train rolled into Truckee. Truckee was a logging town with lots of saloons and bordellos. It gave Bodie a lot of competition for being the toughest town in the West. There were killings almost every night. The Central Pacific stopped for just one hour, long enough for Stryker to use the facilities, buy a sausage biscuit, and a cup of coffee. He'd eaten the sandwich and was about ready to take the last swallow of coffee when a man stomped down the aisle and threw himself onto the bench across from him. He could have been in his mid-thirties. He was decently dressed in a tweed suit with a gambler's black tie. His bland looks just missed being handsome; he was clean-faced with a broad nose that could have been punched in the past. He had hazel eyes and eyebrows that permanently scrunched up above his nose. Stryker wondered if the man shaped the eyebrows by practicing in front of a mirror. Stryker judged him to be no scholar, perhaps one or two levels above dull.

Shit. He'll probably want to talk. Stryker was sorry he'd thrown away the newspaper. He pulled the Stetson down over his brow.

"You wanna know where I'm going?" The man asked the Stetson.

The hat ignored him.

"I'm gonna kill a man."

Stryker tipped the Stetson up with a forefinger.

The man smiled a crooked smile and nodded, satisfied he'd aroused attention from the taciturn Stryker. "You wanna know why I'm gonna shoot him?"

Stryker stared impassively at him, then turned to give more serious attention to the Truckee River flowing alongside the tracks.

The crooked smile waned. "He's a miner in Virginia City. His wife lives in Truckee." The frown disappeared when Stryker swung back to him. "I think he consorted with one of them whores in Virginia City. You know, prostitutes? They got lots of 'em there." The fellow nodded several times to buttress this statement of fact. He went on. "The son of a bitch came to Truckee last month and gave the clap to his wife." He scratched at his crotch, leaned closer to Stryker, and lowered his voice. "What a fucking asshole, don't you think?"

Stryker had to admit he was curious. "That's why you're gonna shoot him."

"Well, no, not exactly." The would-be killer bit his lip, maybe he was thinking something over. He evidently resolved the matter, and the frown returned. He lowered his voice again. "Now I got the durned clap."

Stryker hadn't laughed since he was a small boy in San Francisco, but he had to work hard to stifle one now. Instead, he just said, "That asshole."

The man sat back on the bench. His expression indicated he was satisfied Stryker agreed with killing the asshole.

Stryker let his eyes stay on the fellow for a little bit longer, thinking the man was as dumb as he looked and what kind of woman would fuck him. An ugly visage of a female started to form in his mind, and he quickly shifted away from that. *Just find the painting and get back to*

Pescadero. Maybe go see Morgan, too. "Put a bullet in him." Stryker lowered the Stetson.

That resolved the issue and neither man spoke again. The Central Pacific reached Reno, where the aggrieved man saluted Stryker with a fingertip salute on his hat, and he got off the train to catch the spur train for Virginia City. Stryker watched him walk across the station platform and couldn't help but wonder what would happen when he found the philandering husband. Then he thought about the prostitute and hoped she got cured.

Stryker tried to read the book on art he'd picked up in San Francisco, but he got bored. He found another newspaper left on an empty seat and scanned it between naps as the train rolled across Nevada. The bench across from Stryker remained empty, and he was left alone with his book, the newspapers, and his own thoughts. The train stopped at Humboldt, Winnemucca, Elko, and a bunch of little towns; then it entered Utah during the night. It was just getting light in Salt Lake City. There, he walked the roan, fed it, and watered it. Then he bought coffee before changing over to the Denver and Rio Grande Western Railway for the fourteen-hour trip to Grand Junction. The train steadily climbed into the Rockies as the sun began to set. The beautiful scenery was mostly lost on Stryker except for those few times when the moon broke through clouds and he saw the snow-capped peaks silhouetted against the night sky. The Rockies were every bit as scenic and spectacular as the Sierras, maybe even more so, but the mixed breed didn't care. He was eager to get to Denver and get on with the job he had to do. It wasn't a task he especially relished. He wanted to do it and put it behind him.

The Denver Rio Grande completed its downhill run on the eastern slopes of the Rockies and chugged over level ground. When the train went around the last curve, Stryker saw Denver in the distance. It was a town of around ten thousand that quickly grew because it was located on a rail line shipping cattle eastward for slaughter in the 1880s. Currently, it sought to shred the smell and rowdy reputation of a cow town. The luxurious Windsor Hotel on 18th and Larimer Streets afforded weary travelers first-class accommodations. However, the Brown Palace, which was under construction, would top the Windsor when it opened. The Tabor Grand Opera House provided first-class performances with its fabulous chandelier hanging high above its parquet floor, fifteen-hundred velvet seats, and the finest accouterments.

The train pulled into the Denver Union Station, located on 17th and Wynkoop Streets in downtown Denver. It was around noon that Stryker got directions to the Windsor Hotel, saddled the roan, walked it down the wooden ramp leading out of the livestock car, and climbed on for the four-block ride.

The grand entrance to the five-story, four-hundred-room gothic Windsor Hotel was on Larimer Street. Instead of letting an attendant take the roan to the horse barn on Arapahoe Street, Stryker rode around the corner to the stable. He stabled the roan and made his way along a connecting corridor to the hotel, where he passed a palatial marble bath with Turkish, Russian, and Roman pools. He walked through the noisy gambling hall to the marbled-floor lobby. Around the opulent lobby, a barber shop, a hairdresser, and a restaurant where chefs prepared sumptuous meals with choice meats from its own farm were situated. Wild game was also provided by local hunters. Large chandeliers hung in the lobby that sparkled in the sunlight streaming through side windows. Built by an English firm, under the direction of James Duff, they brought in the finest wood and craftsmen to adorn its features and decorated the interior with raised wallpaper, laced curtains and drapes, and imported furniture. It wasn't the Palace Hotel, but it was the finest hotel between St. Louis and San Francisco.

Stryker walked up to the front desk. "Here to see Marie Mackay," he said to the desk clerk.

"And who might you be, sir?" Came the reply from the smartly dressed young man in a blue pin-striped suit with black, slicked-back hair. The name tag read "Werner" in white letters. His cheeks had the first signs of alcohol-induced rosacea. Werner smiled sarcastically and wore a pink carnation in the lapel buttonhole.

"Stryker." Right away he didn't care for the clerk. The pink flower alone was enough to piss him off, let alone his smart-ass mouth.

"Does she know she knows you?" A scowl replaced the clerk's smile.

"Her husband, John, sent me. Tell her that." Stryker's pale eyes narrowed.

"One moment, sir." Rather than stay behind the desk and attempt to withstand Stryker's withering glare, Werner retreated to a small room behind him where he used a speaking tube to call Mrs. Mackay's room. A few moments later, he returned to an impatient mixed breed. "By the way, here is a telegram for you." He handed the message typed on yellow paper to Stryker.

It read "Van Gogh may have promise. Some paintings were reported to be quite good. E. Holden."

"Mrs. Mackay will meet with you in the reading room, sir." The clerk pointed an open palm to a room where bookshelves, lamp tables, and stuffed chairs were visible through an open doorway. "It's right across the lobby. She asked that you wait for her in there."

"How long's the wait?" Stryker asked.

Werner recoiled, looking startled. Evidently, he hadn't expected such insolence directed at Mrs. Mackay. "I'm sure she will come down shortly, sir," he retorted. "And, sir, men don't normally wear guns in the hotel," he added, eying the Peacemaker on Stryker's hip.

"Give me a room, a good one. Put it on Mackay's bill," Stryker ordered, resting his hand on the Colt. He hadn't intended to use the .44, but no one was going to take it from him either. "Go back and tell Mrs. Mackay she has twenty minutes, then get me the room. Do it now." Stryker figured a telegram would be urgently sent to John Mackay, who probably paid his wife's room charges. He also figured he'd be assigned the room. Stryker waited patiently at the desk for ten minutes before the clerk returned. After all, the fellow had to make two contacts.

"Your key, sir. Room *432*." The emboldened number was stamped black on a polished brass key. "I'm sure you'll find it quite satisfactory. Would you like anything to eat or drink while you wait for Mrs. Mackay?"

"No." Stryker slipped the key into his shirt pocket and headed for the library.

"Who is that man?" another desk clerk asked, coming over to stand beside Werner. His name tag read "Oliver."

"Don't know. The Mackay woman told me to give him what he wants," Werner said, watching Stryker walk across the lobby.

"Mean looking cuss–those eyes 'o his. . . shit! I thought he was gonna shoot you!" Oliver watched Stryker until he could no longer see him in the library. He turned to Werner. "I'd give him what he wants."

"Yeah."

Stryker was perusing a book on philosophy by Fredrich Nietzsche when Marie Mackay joined him.

"Mister Stryker?" She was five feet behind him when she spoke. Shocked by his appearance, she stepped back when he turned around. "You wanted to see me?"

"Mrs. Mackay, I reckon," Stryker said, putting the book back on the shelf. He turned around to face the woman who wore a fleecy navy-blue dress that draped down to the tops of her black pumps. A starched white collar hugged her neck as if it held up her head. The horn-rimmed glasses she wore lay part-way down her nose. Stryker's first thought was, *why she didn't fix the damn things*. A little past her prime maybe. A few years younger and a few pounds lighter she could have been somewhat fetching. He tipped the front of the Stetson with a forefinger.

"Yes, are you a lawman?" Mrs. Mackay asked.

"No."

"A private detective?"

"No."

"Why did my husband send you out here, then?"

"He wants the painting back."

"I see." A hint of a smile cracked her lips. "Call me Marie."

"All right, Marie. Sit." Stryker motioned with an open palm to one of the reading chairs. He sat opposite her with a small round table holding a lamp between them. "Now tell me about the painting. I want to know what it looks like, when and where you last saw it, who knew you had it, its value, and lastly, I want to know about the artist."

Marie straightened the folds of the dress draped over her knees. "It's a painting of yellow plastered buildings on a street corner presumably in Southern France. The yellow house on the corner is two-story. The house beside it looks to be a café. The one behind is four stories high, I think.

There are a few people on the sidewalks. A child could have painted them. The last time I saw it, it was in my hotel room. The hotel maid, Sophia, who cleaned my room, probably saw it on the dresser." Marie scrunched her nose under the glasses and said, "Couldn't be worth much. He, the artist I mean, has only sold one painting I heard, and he's supposed to have made two-thousand drawings."

"What do you know about him?" Stryker asked.

"Not much, only what Rachel told me. How was your train ride?"

"Took three days. Met a few folks. What did Rachel tell you about van Gogh?"

"She said he worked hard at painting, but he couldn't support himself with it. As I said, he only sold one of his paintings.[2] His brother paid for all his living expenses. For a while, he paid Gauguin's too, Paul Gauguin, another painter who lived with Van Gogh in the yellow house for a while." Mrs. Mackay stopped talking and waved down a hotel attaché.

The staff member, a gray-haired man wearing a red uniformed jacket with purple epaulets and maroon trousers, stopped at the library entrance. His name tag read "Wilson." Wilson bowed and straightened. "Yes ma'am?"

"Will you bring me a glass of chilled lemonade, please?" She turned to Stryker. "What would you like, Stryker?"

"Coffee–black."

"Yes, ma'am." The attaché spun on his heels and left.

"Now, where was I? Oh yes, Rachel said van Gogh described himself as a socialist. Are you familiar with what that is, Stryker?"

"An asshole."

"Well, yes. I suppose that describes it. Someone who seeks to live off another person's money," Marie stiffly said.

"I met a couple while back," Stryker growled. "Fed 'em to lions[3]."

Laughing, Marie said, "Metaphorically, of course." She used a ten-dollar word, and then probably thinking Stryker didn't know what it meant, tried to explain. "What I mean is–"

"I know what you mean," Stryker interrupted. "Lions ate 'em."

Mrs. Mackay didn't recoil abruptly, but she did sit back a bit. It could have been because of a grisly visage of lions eating two people or Stryker's language skills. Maybe it was both. "Were the people dead first?" Marie stammered.

"The woman was dead and partially eaten before I got there. Threw the man in with the cats, and they killed him. The woman had gotten too close to the cage, and I threw what was left of her in with the man. Cats hadn't been fed."

Marie took a few moments to think about what Stryker just told her. Finally, she asked, "Are you normally a dangerous man, Mister Stryker?" His looks most likely already conveyed that to her.

"Tell me more about this van Gogh. Why would someone steal a worthless painting?"

"He is also mentally deranged. Rachel spoke as if he sometimes scared her." Marie studied Stryker's features for a loose moment, wondering the same thing about the mixed breed. She collected herself and continued. "I guess he feels possessed by demons he couldn't control as he grew older. She told me he cut off part of his ear with a razor and gave it to her for safekeeping. 'Safekeep a bloody ear!' she screamed at me. She didn't say what she did with it–probably threw it away. Anyway, his paintings… some say he had talent. His brush strokes were often unique, but he reportedly paints really fast and his work seems rushed to critics. Believe me, I researched the man and sought out information about his art, hoping that I'd find out I bought something of real value from Rachel. Now I doubt it. I don't know what I was going to do with the painting. Doesn't matter, anyway. Find the damn thing for John so we can give it back to the van Gogh family. I wish I'd never seen it!"

"What did you pay for it?"

"Ten Francs; about thirty dollars, I guess."

Stryker figured Mrs. Mackay had had about enough at this point, but he wasn't finished. What about the Sophia woman?"

"She doesn't know anything. I'm kind of tired of questions, Stryker. Here come our drinks."

The attaché served the drinks on a red and gold tray with a silver coffee pitcher, a glass of lemonade, a cup and saucer, and cream and sugar for coffee–even though the cream and sugar weren't asked for. Thoughtful service by a first-class hotel.

"Thank you, Wilson," Mrs. Mackay said. Wilson set the tray down, poured the coffee, and handed over their drinks, the glass of lemonade first.

Stryker nodded his thanks, taking the coffee.

"We through here, Mister Stryker?" Mrs. Mackay asked after taking a long sip of lemonade. She patted her mouth with a napkin.

"What else was taken from the room?" Stryker asked.

"Jewelry pieces, seven in all," Marie said. "Expensive, I don't have anything cheap," she added quickly. "I would like those back as well, of course.

"Find someone else to get your jewelry back," Stryker said. "I want to talk with Sophia."

"Why?" Marie hesitated and then said, "Oh, all right. I'll tell her you want to talk with her. Where?" Marie set the glass on the tray and rose to her feet.

"Room *432*. I'll be there in twenty minutes and waiting for her." Stryker had gotten to his feet as well and tipped the Stetson as a salutation.

If Mrs. Mackay had an issue with Stryker being on the same floor as her, she kept it to herself. She said nothing more before leaving Stryker. Probably cause the man seemed capable of almost anything, and anything included murder. It wasn't long after that meeting that she decided to leave for San Francisco. "That man is unpleasant," she said aloud to herself.

Stryker refilled his cup and walked from the reading room to the lobby. The strong aroma of grilled steak wafted from the dining room and he ambled toward it, sipping coffee along the way. He peaked inside. The room was spacious with white tablecloths, large comfortable chairs, and waiters in white tuxedos. It was an elegant place to fill one's belly. He sipped more coffee, stepped away from the dining room, and faced the expansive lobby. A stenciled name above an open doorway led to the Bonanza Bar, which was only used by hotel gamblers. Near it, a similar doorway opened into the Cattleman's Room. It allowed public gambling. Close by those two rooms, a stairway dubbed the "suicide stairs" led to a gambling hall on the fifth floor where the very rich had to pony up at least $5,000 to play. Many a fortune was lost up there and despondent losers sometimes flung themselves down the stairs. Stryker returned to his mission and why he was in Denver. *If Sophia knows nothing, where do I start with this?*

Polished and gleaming, a wide set of stairs of dark wood, probably mahogany, led to the upper guest rooms. He gave the coffee cup to a passing staff member and headed for the stairs. No rising room in this hotel, he climbed up four flights to the fourth floor. When he mounted the last steps, he was surprised to see a woman waiting down the hall near, if he counted the doors right, room *432*. She wasn't in uniform. He walked down to meet her.

"Sophia," Stryker said as a greeting.

"Yes, sir."

Sophia wore a plain yellow dress with no belt. She was maybe five feet high and perhaps a little stout for his taste. She wore her prematurely gray hair swept back with a white kerchief. Elk-horned glasses rested on her round rosy cheeks and accented a very nervous smile. Stryker guessed her age to be mid to late-thirties. He slipped the key in the lock and opened the door. He held it open for her to enter, but she held back.

"Mrs. Mackay said you wanted to see me. She didn't tell me what you wanted." The smile had faded.

With more of her talking, Stryker realized Sophia had a slight French accent. *Okay.* He figured that moved her up a couple notches. French accent on a girl seemed to make her more attractive, but that only went so far. An overweight woman with protruding nose hair and warts can't be helped. West European accents for the most part are attractive in girls. *Not so Russian or Czechoslovakian*, Stryker thought. For some reason, Slavic women sound capable of castrating a man if he pissed 'em off. "I want to ask you a few questions," Stryker said.

"And then what?"

"Then you leave." Stryker had a hunch Marie could have ordered Sophia to do just about anything and she would have complied, unwillingly perhaps, but the girl probably needed her job. And Mrs. Mackay was a powerful woman. Women like Sophia had few options to make a living. Stryker didn't want to take advantage of the girl, though. Besides, he wasn't in the mood.

Sophia stepped inside the room.

The room had raised velvet gold and black wallpaper, a queen bed with a thick gold-colored quilt, black fur rugs of different sizes on the floor, a desk and chair, and two stuffed chairs for reading under one of three wall lamps. There was not a full bathroom. There was a small separate room with an upright chest that had a wash bowl, a pitcher of water, and towels. Stryker glanced around the room. It was not his taste.

"Sit there," Stryker said, waving at a stuffed chair.

Sophia marched to the chair and sat. If a person can sit at attention, she did. Her back was straight, and her hands were on her knees that were clasped together under the yellow dress.

Stryker sat in the other chair. He leaned back in a more relaxed position. "What do you know about the painting stolen from Mrs. Mackay?"

"Nothing. Someone stole it. I don't know who," Sophia replied defensively.

"Other thefts at this hotel," Stryker queried in a statement.

Sophia seemed confused until she realized he'd asked her a question. "Well, yes."

"Tell me." Stryker leaned forward.

"Things are taken…" Sophia hesitated.

"Go on," Stryker ordered. She had more to tell. It was obvious.

"Mrs. Mackay asked me to give you whatever you asked. I didn't know you would ask about stolen things. I don't take what don't belong to me." Sophia scooted to the edge of the chair. She eyed the door.

"But you do know who might be pilfering, Sophia," Stryker said.

"Mister, even though Mrs. Mackay told me to… and you're her friend… I guess?" The girl scrunched the folds of her dress with nervous hands. "If they know I said something, I'd be in danger," she quickly blurted.

Stryker's face hardened. "You're in danger now."

Sophia scooted away from him, not back in the chair, away from him.

"You won't make it to the door, girl."

Sophia hesitated and then she settled into the chair. "All right. You won't say where you got it, and you'll let me leave afterward?"

"Yes," Stryker said, nodding.

"Down the street, there's a saloon and gambling hall called The Tivoli Club. A man named Soapy Smith owns it. He runs just about everything in town. They say the sheriff is on his payroll. If he gets word that I told…"

"He won't. Now go on," Stryker cut in.

"Nobody will protect me," Sophia added, apparently attempting to make sure he knew that.

"Understood."

"I know what you're thinking, mister," Sophia said. "You think you could protect me, but you can't. There's too many of them." She eyed the Peacemaker. "Are you any good with that?"

"Yes."

Sophia shifted her attention away from the Colt and back to the man wearing it. "I think maybe you are. Soapy got the name for selling soap bars with some of them supposed to have money wrapped up in them. It's well known only his own men won the prizes, no one else. Besides gambling and drinking, he sells fake stock certificates, fake jewelry, and other fake stuff in the cigar shop next to the Tivoli. He's a con man, Mister…"

"Stryker."

"Mister Stryker, he's the vilest of swindlers with no shred of a conscience. He also has a very violent temper. That's why I'm afraid of him. He'll kill me."

"You think stolen items from the hotel end up in his shop," Stryker said.

"And I didn't tell you that."

"Sprinkle a few genuine pieces in with the fake, and they look legitimate too." Stryker sat back in the chair. "And out-of-town hotel victims leave Denver before their property is shown in the shops," Stryker continued.

Sophia nodded.

Stryker rose and went to the door. He opened it and leaned out. After looking up and down the hallway, he turned to Sophia and said, "You can go."

The maid rose from the bed, gave Stryker a wilted smile, and left the room.

Stryker waited a good thirty minutes before he followed her out and went downstairs. "Which way to the Tivoli Club?" Stryker asked Werner at the front desk.

"Go left out the front and down Larimer Street. Not far, sir."

Stryker turned to walk out.

"Sir, you may want to leave your gun here with us." Werner called out to Stryker. "Not a good idea to walk in that place with your gun. The saloon guards have shotguns, and they don't hesitate to use 'em. Sorry, sir. Just a warning."

Stryker paused to reflect. "All right." He unstrapped the gun belt. "I'll be back for it."

He walked out of the Windsor Hotel and headed down 17th Street to The Tivoli Club. It began to get dark and he could hear music coming from the saloon a half block away.

A small sign hung from a steel bar outside read "Caveat Emptor," buyer beware. *An odd warning*, Stryker thought as he approached the double doorway. Suddenly, the doors flung open, and the sound of a throaty male singer with female backup voices, and an accompanying band blared through the opening. Then out came a man, half dragged-half carried, by two burly men who threw him onto the street. The two men glanced at Stryker and went back inside. They wore black suits with white shirts and black western ties. Their guest whom they'd escorted outside, had on a suit as well, but he was a bit rumpled and somewhat disheveled. *Must be an upscale joint*, Stryker mused to himself. He opened a door and went in.

Once inside, he saw the male singer with a guitar and a five-piece band. The three-foot stage was maybe thirty paces away to his right. A support column stood between him and the stage, and he couldn't see all the band members. It didn't matter. Stryker wasn't there for the music. He did hear it though, guitars, drums, piano, and horns–the towering horn blowing was unusual for a saloon. He continued surveying the room while he listened. The Tivoli was packed with gamblers and drinkers. The bar was straight ahead with plenty of card tables in between for gamblers and drinkers. Every table was taken and no space was available at the bar without him having to push his way in. Men outnumbered women twenty to one. Many western saloons outlawed women altogether, but Tivoli allowed them. Most were prostitutes but some females weren't. They must have been single women who sought a rich man who might want to marry and support them. Women had a hard life. The official gambling room was upstairs where faro, roulette, and poker lightened men's wallets. The Tivoli wasn't opulent, but it did have a few accouterments, such as a long, polished bar with fancy brass trappings, felt tables for gambling, a deli for sandwiches, and the stage band. Soapy also had multiple American flags inside and out, as if to triumph his patriotism. Lanterns on the wallpapered walls and wagon wheel lanterns hung from the ceiling, providing adequate lighting. There was enough light to read a man's cards in his hands anyway. Soapy was proud of the band. Usually, bars in the old west only had pianos. Some didn't even have that.

Stryker stepped farther in and stood by the wall just as the lead singer and the band struck up a new song.

"It was snowin' the night I rode into town
Freezin' cold, it lay on the ground
Down the street, I heard a sad melody
Comin' from this place they call the Tivoli

Well, I stepped inside and stood by the bar
A dark-haired girl sang and played the guitar
I saw hookers and hustlers, and sinful revelry
Comin' from this place called Club Tivoli

There's whiskey, card cheaters, and evil women
All of 'em here to take your winnins
And if the booze and hustlers don't kill you quickly
The women will, down at the bar called Tivoli

> Well sold my gun, and I sold my ring
> Just to hear that little girl sing
> Don't care who you are, you can end up dead
> Touch that girl and get a belly full of lead
> Yeah, get your belly full of lead."

Stryker moved from behind the column and took a second glance at the band. On the stage behind the male vocalist, a girl sang and played the guitar. She had dark hair and she was pretty, and… familiar.

Raelyn.

Stryker didn't recognize her at first. Her hair hung straight and stringy. She wore lots of make-up, and she was much thinner. To be sure, he maneuvered closer to the stage to see if she would recognize him. She did. She stopped for a moment and then continued to sing.

When she looked at him again, Stryker nodded toward a side door by the stage. A painted exit sign above it suggested it led outside. He wove his way back through the tables to the front door. Turning left, he found the alley where he figured the exit door would be. He walked down the alley. It was dark and he was almost at the doorway before he'd found it. Ten minutes later, Raelyn came out the door.

"Stryker, what are you doing here?" she whispered.

No one else was in the alley, and he wondered why she felt the need to whisper. He suspected she wasn't supposed to talk to the customers.

"Business." Stryker didn't whisper.

"I guess you're surprised to find me here," she said stoically, sounding as if she were ashamed.

"I didn't know you played the guitar."

Raelyn cracked a weak smile. Stryker could barely see it in the darkness. "Soapy said I had talent, and he offered me a job."

"Want to ask you a few questions."

"About why I'm at this place?"

"No, trying to recover a stolen painting."

"I gotta go back in." Raelyn spun around for the door.

It opened before she reached it. One of the guards Stryker saw throwing the man out of the saloon appeared in the doorway. He was the bigger one with a heavy beard. He came out and slammed the door behind him.

"Who you talkin' out here, girl?"

"An old friend, Max. He's no trouble." Raelyn talked fast and she flattened her hands on Max's chest to hold him back.

Max shoved her aside and swung a leaded baton at Stryker's head.

It was too dark for Stryker to see the baton, but he got a glimpse of Max's arm movement. He stepped back and sideways, lifting an arm to block. He reached for the sai. The baton glanced off his shoulder, grazing the top of his head.

Max squared himself for another blow, holding the baton at the ready.

Stryker flipped the sai in his hand. Lunging forward, he smashed the pummel against Max's forehead. He was stunned, but the big man remained on his feet. Stryker rotated the sai again and swung in a tight circle, striking the middle tine against the carotid artery on Max's neck.

Max staggered backward. Stryker went with him, twisting the sai a quarter turn, he plunged a side prong through the bouncer's windpipe. Max grabbed at his throat and dropped to his knees. The baton slipped from his hand, and he fell forward.

"He's gonna be really mad when he wakes up," Raelyn warned. The killing blow happened quickly. It was dark. She failed to see the sai. Max didn't either.

"C'mon." Stryker took Raelyn by the elbow and guided her toward the alley front.

"Where's Floyd and Priscilla?" Stryker growled. He wasn't in a good mood. Killing Max most likely meant trouble. But leaving him alive would have complicated things, too. He felt the resentment toward Raelyn rise in his throat. He wouldn't have killed Max were it not for her. Not that he regretted that; he wanted to get information about the painting without being conspicuous. *What the hell was she doing with a gangster like Soapy Smith anyway? What to do with the woman now?* Stryker hoped to find out from Raelyn where the gang kept stolen merchandise, so he needed her, at least for the time being. *But wait.* Every once in a while, the mixed breed got a bright idea.

CHAPTER SIX

"We'll go back to the Windsor Hotel for dinner." Stryker thought the girl needed food. "And then after that, I want you to introduce me to Smith. What's his real first name?" They emerged from the alley and Stryker led her up Larimer Street.

They'd walked past the entrance to the Tivoli Club where Raelyn erupted. "What! Are you crazy?" She stopped and turned to Stryker. "I should go back now," she said, jerking her arm from his grasp.

"His real name," Stryker demanded. He grabbed her arm again.

"Jefferson, I think. Why?"

"I need to show him respect."

"Show Soapy respect? That's a new one. Why are we going to the hotel?"

"I want to talk to you."

"That's it?" Raelyn sounded as if she suspected Stryker wanted more than talk.

"I don't care who you've been fucking." Stryker immediately regretted that one. He needed information from her. *Shit.* "A grieving woman will sometimes turn to someone to ease the pain or help support her if she's desperate. Maybe she makes a bad decision. Never know. Can't really blame her, or you, I reckon."

"You're not a woman. How would you know?" Raelyn pulled her arm away again.

"You never told me where Floyd and Priscilla are."

"They stayed on the train, going east. I didn't have the money. I refused to take any more from them. They'd done enough. They helped pay for the funeral. I told 'em I wanted to stay in Denver. Never told 'I was out of money. There, dammit! Think what you want."

They walked the block and a quarter to the Windsor without further discussion of money or poor decisions. A doorman greeted them at the door. Stryker guided Raelyn to the front desk where he collected his gun belt, and they crossed the lobby to the dining room.

"Two for dinner," Stryker told the maître d' wearing a white tuxedo jacket. "That table over there," Stryker said, pointing at a table for two against the back wall, rejecting the maître d's choice.

"Yes, sir." The maitre d' escorted them to the table by the wall. "Ma'am." He pulled out a chair for Raelyn. Stryker seated himself. A waiter was waved over.

"Wine for the lady, beer for me," Stryker said to the waiter.

"I could have ordered myself," Raelyn huffed after the waiter gave them menus and walked away.

"Smith collects stolen valuables and then sells them in his cigar store," Stryker said, ignoring her grousing. "Where does he keep the stuff until he puts it out for sale?"

"I didn't know he had stolen property. He never shared that with me. I haven't worked for him that long, you know. Why you asking? He steal something from you?"

"Not from me. A French painting of a yellow house. Have you seen it?"

"No, and if Soapy has it, he won't tell you. You'd have to beat it out of him, and I don't think he's ever alone much."

"Shit! How many men work for Soapy?"

"Eight or ten in the saloon, I think. Outside, I don't know. The sheriff and deputies, and most of the politicians in this town are on his payroll, though."

"In the saloon, who's his main man?"

"That would be Max."

"Smith is now short one man. I want you to introduce me as a close friend. I'm gonna take Max's place."

"Did you kill him?" Raelyn scrunched her face. "You really are crazy, aren't you? You kill Max and you want Soapy to hire you? Damn, Stryker."

"What you want for dinner?"

Stryker and Raelyn picked up menus written in flourished script and read through the day's listings. The menus were revised daily to reflect fresh and exotic offerings–oysters on the half shell, baked flounder, a la Chamborg, boiled leg of lamb with young carrots, filets of rabbit larded with mushrooms, and roast Baron of beef with Yorkshire pudding were just some of the mouth-watering temptations. Assorted sweet brandies and ample confectionaries, pies, and multiple flavors of ice creams completed the dining experience for those who had sweet tooths.

"Lamb, I guess."

The waiter returned with wine and beer. Stryker ordered the lamb for Raelyn, and steak for himself. When their meals arrived, they ate without saying much. Raelyn did remark with weak enthusiasm, how good her lamb was. As she cut into it, an unruly strand of hair fell across her face, and with a quick swipe of her hand, she swept it back behind her ear. That made her prominent cheekbone more noticeable, and Stryker liked prominent cheekbones. Beneath the protruding facial bones, her cheeks appeared somewhat sallow. He hadn't noticed her eyes, and he couldn't see them now as she looked down at her plate. He thought he remembered them as being dark, but he wasn't sure. Stryker eyed her hands. He studied them while she chewed. She was busy arranging and cutting around the lamb bone and didn't notice him staring. Her hands were thin, tanned, and delicate, and he imagined them working the strings on the guitar. The guitar he didn't know she played. She was a wisp of a girl now. Raelyn had lost a lot of weight, and he wondered if it was due to her grieving over her dead husband. It had only been a few days, though.

Even after saying it was good, Raelyn took her time cutting the meat into small bites, acting as if she wasn't all that hungry. Stryker couldn't quite figure the girl out. For all he knew, she could be smoking opium, and that's why she looked the way she did.

"How long have you played the guitar?" Stryker asked when she caught him looking at her.

"I learned when I was little. My mother wanted me to play the violin, but my brother was learning guitar. I used to sneak time on it. I liked the guitar better than the violin," Raelyn replied in a monotone.

Stryker would have preferred a girl play the violin, but he kept it to himself. "Let's go see Soapy"

Raelyn had been hovering the fork over the lamb, staring at it. She opened her fingers and the fork clanged to the plate. "Okay."

They scooted away from the table and got to their feet. Stryker waved the waiter to their table. "Put it on room *432*."

A cloudy night greeted them when they stepped out of the Windsor. Lantern posts and lights from windows lit patches of the walkway. Clamor from the opened door of the *Tivoli Club* grew louder as they got closer to the saloon.

Stryker draped his hand over the Peacemaker and loosened it in the holster. Saloons in those days were notoriously violent, and the *Tivoli* built in early1888 was dubbed the "slaughter pen" by the *Rocky Mountain News*. Going into the Club, he wouldn't turn over his gun. Stryker hadn't gone undercover before. He wasn't sure how to act, how to bluff. He'd always dealt with dangerous situations with gun and blade– violently. Tonight, he would try a different strategy, and if that didn't work, he'd resort to his usual bloody way of doing things.

Stryker held the door for Raelyn to enter first; after all, he had been an officer and a gentleman at one time. He followed her in. The saloon was even more crowded than before, and cigar smoke hung over the room like a blanket. Being later in the evening, drinkers had ratcheted up the volume.

"Is Max around?" Raelyn yelled out to no one in particular.

Clever girl. She wants to know if his body has been discovered. Stryker searched for guns pointed their way.

"Hey, the band's been looking for you," the bartender shouted back.

Raelyn made her way between beer tables to the bar. "I know, Russell. I'm looking for Max."

"Ain't seen 'im," the barkeep said. Wearing a white shirt with green armbands, he picked up a beer mug and swiped it with a cloth.

"Well, what about Soapy? Where's he?" Raelyn asked.

"Miss, don't you think you should get back up there with the band?" Russell nodded toward the stage. The lead singer had seen Raelyn by now, but he kept singing.

"He's here, upstairs I reckon." The bartender followed that up with, "That man behind you wanna drink?"

"No, he wants a job. We'll go find Jeff. Maybe later, if he gets hired and makes some money." Raelyn winked and laughed.

This girl is good. Must have been a good actress. Stryker tipped the Stetson at Russell and followed Raelyn to the stairway. The serious gambling happened on the second floor. It was the reason Smith spent most of his time up there. He wanted to keep his eye on the big money changing hands, usually from customers to his. The business office sat at the far end of the gambling floor. Raelyn failed to see Soapy anywhere and whispered to Stryker, "He's probably in his office." She took off weaving between the crowded tables toward the back.

Stryker saw four guards standing by the walls with shotguns. They took notice of him as well. Three-fourths of the table games were faro and that's where most of the boisterous men crowded, trying their luck. A few monte, poker, and roulette tables were also spread about. Men threw down large wads of cash, whooping on wins, cursing on losses. The raucous gambling hall required a lot of attention. When the guards saw it was Raelyn leading Stryker to Soapy's office, they went back to watching the tables.

The second-floor gambling hall was huge, taking up much of the floor space. It was decorated with American flags, paintings, and arti-facts. Smith must have figured men wouldn't mind losing their asses in such *patriotic* surroundings. Maybe he was right. Soapy Smith may have looked like a country bumkin, but he was one smart crook. He once testi-fied he was doing people in Denver a big favor, claiming gamblers in his saloon lost their money so quickly they would swear off gambling for good. A few probably did.

Dealers stood in cut-outs at the rectangular faro tables, dealing the cards. They wore pin-striped shirts and straw hats. Some wore garters on their sleeves. In all, Stryker quickly counted thirty-six faro games with gamblers, all men, seated opposite the dealer. In front of the men, stacks of chips and poker cards lay face-up. The object of the game was for the dealer to deal them matching cards. Of course, standing by the players with the largest pile of chips, the prostitutes who wore frilly dresses, feather boas, lots of make-up, and very wide and colorful straw hats. Stryker figured the seven closed doors lining the far wall led to pleasure dens. Gambling hall owners sought to keep winners in the house. Smith got his cut from the soiled doves too. All revenue sources led to him.

The door to the office was open. Not for a "welcome, come on in" purpose, rather he wanted to have the dealers and gamblers think he always watched them. And he did.

Raelyn entered the office first. Stryker came in behind her. Soapy sat in a high-backed leather swivel-tilt chair behind a tan oak desk. Two empty straight-back chairs were in front. Two wooden filing cabinets were behind the desk, and there was a cot along the left wall. Hanging on the pine-paneled wall behind the desk, a painting showed off Soapy on his horse. Stryker noticed the cot was fully made up. Stryker figured the closed door in a corner of the wall behind the desk led to outside stairs. Soapy wore a black suit, white shirt, and a western tie, and he had his boots up on the desk. He talked to two men standing beside the desk. They both wore black pin-striped pants, white shirts, and black leather vests. They also had black leather gun belts with holstered Colt .45s. Raelyn's entrance interrupted their meeting.

"Raelyn, what you need, darlin'?" Smith said, showing surprise at seeing her. He swung his feet to the floor.

"Meet my cousin, Neville Stryker. He wants a job."

Smith offered a wide-toothed grin and leaned forward, resting his elbows on the desk. The two men swung around to face Raelyn and Stryker.

"Well, I don't know 'bout that, honey. Mister Stryker, what kind of work do you do?" Smith asked, shifting his attention to Stryker.

Stryker stepped in front of Raelyn before answering. "I keep peace in saloons."

"I'm awfully sorry, Stryker, but we have enough men for that now." Smith eyed Stryker's Peacemaker and added, "Maybe you can come back later, and I'll see what I can do." He then glanced at his men who were staring at Stryker.

"I want Max's job," Stryker said.

"You've met Max?" Smith asked. The wide smile faded to a puzzled frown.

"Yes."

"I don't think Max would like that," Smith said. "I wouldn't either. He's my best man."

"He was second best tonight. Raelyn, close the door." Stryker dropped his hand to the Peacemaker.

Raelyn hesitated and then closed the door.

"Why'd you close the door, Stryker?" Smith glanced at his men, a telling sign for them to prepare for gunplay.

"Don't want *reason* to leave the room," Stryker said. He also didn't want another guard coming in behind him, and if one did come in, he'd be warned by the door opening.

"What you mean 'second best'?"

"He attacked me in the alley, and I killed him."

Soapy's two men started to make a play for their guns.

But before they could draw, Stryker had the Peacemaker pointed at Smith's chest. Stryker's draw was smooth and very quick—with an ominous hammer click.

"I can put three bullets in you before they shoot. Tell your men to stand down."

"Hold your fire, boys." Smith raised a palm toward his men.

"We were just talking, and Max came out swinging a club. Stryker had to defend himself, Soapy." Raelyn stepped beside *her cousin*.

"Zeke, go see about Max," Soapy ordered. "By the saloon door to the alley?" He looked at Raelyn.

"Yes," she answered.

Zeke quick-stepped to the door.

"Zeke!" Smith yelled after him. "Tell the men don't come in. Gaver," Soapy called to his other man. "Stand outside the door. Don't let anyone in," he ordered, waving Gaver toward the door. "You can put your gun away, Stryker. Have a seat."

Stryker holstered the Colt, pulled out a chair for Raelyn, and then one for himself. They sat and waited for Soapy to speak. His fake smile reappeared.

"You know, Stryker, maybe we *can* work out an arrangement. Where you hail from?" He shoved his black felt hat back from his forehead. Smith often did that to make himself look more friendly, likable… and stupid, as if he were a man who could be taken advantage of. Of course, he was none of those.

"My folks moved away from Raelyn's before I was born. I grew up in San Francisco. Stryker figured telling a lie to the king of liars wasn't lying–*negative times a negative is positive*. Besides, he had no idea where Raelyn was born.

"My parents stayed in Philadelphia like I'd told you," Raelyn quickly intercepted. "And I came out to San Francisco with my acting troupe this year."

"Where you staying in Denver?" Smith probed Stryker.

"The Windsor. A wealthy woman put me up for a while."

"What are you doing for the woman?" Smith beamed a shit-eatin' grin.

"None of your business."

"I see." A frown ran the grin off.

The door flew open and Zeke came in. He was breathing hard from running. "Max is dead all right."

"The job pays ten dollars a week, Stryker."

"Boss, you ain't gonna really hire this man, are ya?" Zeke asked incredulously.

"Not at ten dollars a week," Stryker said, eying Smith with a steely gaze.

Soapy studied Stryker for several long seconds, not saying anything.

"How much were you paying Max?" Stryker asked.

Soapy glanced at Zeke and thought about telling Stryker "None of your business," but the man across from him was quick with a gun, and instead he said, "Eighteen dollars."

Zeke cleared his throat.

Stryker figured eighteen dollars was a lie.

"I'll work for thirty-five dollars a week, same as you pay the rest of the men."

Soapy started to protest but then realized he'd been outfoxed. "All right. You can start today."

"Welcome to the Tivoli!" Zeke exclaimed, stepping to Stryker's chair and offering a handshake. He spun around and hurriedly left the office with a wide grin on his face. In his haste, he left the door open.

Stryker figured he was in a rush to tell the other men they'd just gotten a raise.

"Thank you, Soapy. You won't regret hiring my cousin," Raelyn said, rising from her chair. "I better go down and join the band. I'm sure they're wondering what happen to me. Good to see you again, Stryker. Do a good job for Soapy." And with that, she leaned down and kissed Stryker on the cheek. "Bye now," she said breezily to both men, and she left the office.

Soapy watched Raelyn leave, studying the woman.

"Tell me about Max's duties, Jefferson," Stryker said, interrupting Soapy's scrutiny. He used the saloon boss's first name. Stryker stayed sitting with an ankle propped on his knee. "I want to do a good job for you."

Jefferson "Soapy" Smith paused before answering, wondering if he'd just hired the man who was going to kill him. He leaned forward, resting his arms on the desk. "Max watched over the men in the saloon downstairs, the gambling up here, and the whores." Soapy waved his hand. "And generally watched over the whole place. Max was my right-hand man. I trusted him, and he was loyal to me. You think you can fill his boots, Stryker?" He showed a big wide, fake grin. But then, Soapy's big wide grins were always fake.

"Sure." Stryker got to his feet. "I'll get familiar with the place." He started toward the door.

"Glad to have you here!" Soapy gushed. He rushed around the desk to shake hands.

Stryker accepted the man's hand, and he allowed his new boss to vigorously jack his hand up and down. Stryker figured the handshake was like the grin, fake. He spun around and walked from the office.

Gaver watched the mixed breed amble past him and over to a faro table. Then he whirled and rushed into the office. "You hired that guy, boss?" Gaver asked, hooking a thumb over his shoulder.

"Yeah, I did." Smith saw Stryker strutting among the card tables. "I hope it wasn't a mistake, though."

"He was pretty quick on the draw," Gaver allowed. Zeke told him about the pay raise, so he wasn't gonna criticize the new hire.

"Yep." Soapy returned to his chair where he sat studying a paper weight. "He sure as hell was."

"You trust him?"

"No."

Stryker found Zeke downstairs talking with the bartender. "Zeke, I reckon word's out I'm taking Max's place."

Zeke nodded, saying, "Didn't take long."

"Take me around and introduce me to everybody." Stryker was now having second thoughts about the strategy. He had the drop on Soapy. *Should've just stuck the Peacemaker in his gut and demanded the painting.* But what Raelyn told Stryker about Soapy played a part in his actions. However, he might get a chance later to put a razor on his throat and find out how much he valued artwork.

One of the dealers Stryker met was Bat Masterson. As crooked as Soapy was, he was well-liked by the locals. He gave money to charities, churches, and other worthy causes, and he directed most of his scams at out-of-towners. On more than one occasion, he'd set up fake female kidnappings, and then he and his men would rescue the damsels in distress.

Zeke and Stryker made the rounds with introductions on the second floor before heading downstairs. Downstairs was noisy but not compared to the din upstairs. Stryker gave vague answers to questions people asked of him.

When he finished meeting everybody, including the band, Zeke said, "C'mon, I'll show you the cigar shop. Sells cigars, pipes, and a collectible every now and then," Zeke said. "The real action is in back of the store where there's card games. Bascomb, Soapy's brother, runs the store." Thirty-five dollars a week made Zeke more friendly. He led Stryker out of Tivoli's and to the cigar shop.

Inside the store, Zeke came up to Bascomb. "This here is Stryker. He's gonna replace Max."

"I heard Max got killed. I didn't hear how," Bascomb said, eying Stryker with suspicion.

"An accident. Max and Stryker didn't know each other, and it was dark."

"You kill 'im?" Bascomb asked.

"Yeah, and like I told ya. It was a accident, Bascomb," Zeke interjected.

"Okay, Stryker," Bascomb groused. He didn't offer a handshake.

Bascomb didn't sport a beard like his brother, rather he maintained a well-manicured mustache, and he wore his hair short, neatly parted on the side. Bascomb held himself out to be a retired lawyer. His and Soapy's father and several of their uncles were attorneys, and the ruse came easy to Bascomb. Inside the shop, display cases promoted jewelry, pocket watches, stock certificates, land deeds, and assorted artifacts purportedly worth much more than their selling prices. Of course, all of the items were fake. Stryker marveled at the breadth of Soapy's scams. If there was a con to be had, he used it.

"Bascomb, why don't ya take Stryker in back, show him the tables, and introduce him to the boys?" Zeke said.

Zeke waited out front checking over the merchandise while Stryker went with Bascomb to the card room. Much smaller than the Tivoli gambling hall and twice as smoky, the poker room had eight card tables with men seated tightly around them. Others stood waiting to play. Patriotic flags and memorabilia decorated the twenty-by-twenty poker room like the saloon next door. Bascomb pointed at the dealers and said their names, but he didn't introduce Stryker. After that, he brought Stryker back to the front of the shop

Stryker then left Bascomb and strolled around. Bending over the counters, studying the items for sale, making comments on occasion, and then he asked, "Get art paintings in here?"

"We had one in here six months ago," Bascomb replied. "You interested in art, are ya, Stryker?"

"Curious. That's all. Remember what it was?"

Bascomb frowned, squinted his eyes, and cocked his head. "It was of dogs playin' poker."

Stryker stared at Bascomb, not believing the man. Bascomb stared back.

"Let's go, Stryker," Zeke said interrupting the stand-off.

Zeke and Stryker left the store and started back up the sidewalk to Tivoli's.

"Max worked from about dusk to dawn, Stryker. I reckon that'll be your hours too," Zeke said as they came to the alley separating the cigar store and Tivoli's. He was about to say more when a woman's scream came from the dark alleyway.

"Aaaaahhhh! You son-of-bitch! You killed my Max!" The shadow of a woman lunged from the alley with a butcher knife.

"Mable! Dammit!" Zeke tried to grab the short, stout woman and the arm holding the knife. He missed the arm.

Mable sunk the blade into Zeke's shoulder. She was trying to pull it out when Stryker shot her.

"Umph!" Mable expelled air when the .44 slug punched her belly. Part of a kidney blew out the hole in her back. She fell to her knees, and Stryker shot her in the forehead.

Stryker holstered the Peacemaker, knocked Zeke's hand off the knife, and pulled it out. Zeke stared at Mable's body. She was on her back now, and he'd only slightly winced when Stryker extracted the blade. It wasn't very deep.

"God damn, Stryker. Did you have to shoot her?"

"No."

Zeke looked at Stryker and thought about that for a bit. Then he said,

"Soapy doesn't like violence. Gives us a bad name." Zeke shifted attention back to the woman's body. "We should get Jones for her too, I guess. Randall Jones in town here built out the saloon and gambling hall. Does coffins on the side." Zeke rubbed his shoulder. You could tell it was starting to hurt. "Regular undertaker will blab this all over town. Told Gaver to get him for Max. He can make one for the wife now too."

"Get a doctor to look at that shoulder. I'm gonna do my job." Stryker walked on down the sidewalk, leaving Zeke to stare at Mabel's body by himself.

"Right after I find Jones." Zeke called after Stryker. Zeke followed him for half a block and then turned down the alley where Max was killed. "Mean son-of-a-bitch," Zeke muttered under his breath. He rolled up his sleeve to see blood rolling down his arm. Jones and Gaver were loading Max's body into a flatbed wagon.

"Got another one for ya," Zeke said, walking up to Jones. "His wife. Tried to stab Stryker. Got me instead, and Stryker shot her. She's in the next alley over. Pick her up and take 'em both out to bury. We don't want a big fuss over this. Go with him, Gaver." Zeke undid a button on the front of his shirt to act as sling for his injured arm. "I gotta go see about my damn shoulder. Shit, crazy-ass woman." Zeke walked from the alley and headed across the street.

Raelyn was playing the guitar with the band when Stryker entered the saloon. He felt he owed her one, so he tipped the Stetson toward her. He strolled around the saloon a few times and then climbed the stairs to the second floor. A soiled dove accompanying an old timer in his overalls was ascending the stairs behind him. The prostitute appeared well past her prime, but she wore a lot of make-up. Stryker figured if her customer were twenty years younger, she'd probably have to pay him. For now, it looked like a fair trade. On the second floor, it had gotten a lot noisier. Winners whooping. Losers cussing. It was quite a racket.

Stryker walked to the far side of the floor, and one of the four guards carrying shotguns came up to him. "Hey, Soapy wants to see ya." That's all he said. He spun away and returned to his station along the wall.

Stryker crossed the floor to the office. The door was closed. He opened the door and stepped inside. The first thing he noticed was—no

Soapy. Instead, there were five armed men waiting for him, two with shotguns, three with handguns, all pointed his way. One of them wore a badge.

"Hands in the air, Stryker," the short lawman ordered. His badge was pinned on the breast pocket of his black suit. "You even twitch and my deputies will shoot. You're under arrest for the murder of Max Hogan." He nodded toward the man closest to Stryker. "Take his gun, Harley."

Harley stepped behind Stryker. He held a pistol in Stryker's back, and pulled out the Peacemaker.

"Put the cuffs on him, Swede." A six-foot-blonde-headed fellow came from the other side of Stryker and pulled his arms behind him one at a time to put on the handcuffs. The stumpy lawman stepped in front of Stryker and got in his face. "We don't allow your type coming in here, shootin' up the place, and killin' one of our finest, mister."

"Got 'em on him, Bill." Harley said, stepping away from Stryker.

With five guns trained on him, Stryker had allowed the cuffing without a struggle. He glared at the sheriff first and then glanced around at the other men. *All of 'em on Smith's payroll. Shit.*

Two deputies got on both sides of Stryker and gripped his arms above the elbows. They walked him from the office, past the card tables, and down the stairs to the saloon. Few people even gave the six men glances. Most were consumed with gambling. Those who did eye them did so briefly and went back to the games. Stryker wasn't the first man to be escorted from the place. Once outside Tivoli, it was a short walk to the Denver jail.

Same as a typical western city jail, the sheriff's office was in front, and a rear door led to cells in the back. Six heavily barred cells, three on each side, were all empty. They put Stryker in the first one on the right.

Stryker had been behind bars before. He hated it. He guessed everyone did. They didn't take off the cuffs either. He'd often thought if he had to spend his life in prison, a cage, he'd rather be shot, or in this case, hanged. He sat on the cot and tried to think of a way out of the jail. Nothing immediately came to mind.

Two fruitless hours later, he reclined on the cot. Even if he busted out of the jail, he'd still need to find the painting–if the job were to be completed. To Stryker, it was a silly mission in the first place, retrieving the artwork to preserve honor. He could care less about another man's honor. His own code was what he lived by, and finding the damn painting was within that code, finishing what he started, and keeping his word.

He lay back on the cot, tired of trying to figure a way out of jail. His mind wandered to memories of Leigh. The singer in San Francisco brought them back. The brief period he was married to Leigh was the only time he thought he was close to being happy. It was useless to think about it. Still, it was good. Leigh was good. He missed her. He had good memories with her, too few though. If he didn't fall asleep, he could maybe recall some of the good ones. They appeared during times like these, times of despair. But if he slept, the nightmares came, the ones where his wife was bloodied and dying from the exploded artillery round. His last image of her still haunted him. He'd knelt by her and lifted her head. She opened her eyes and said his name on blood bubbling from her lips. He'd try to shut that out now and remember something good with Leigh.

CHAPTER SEVEN

It was a pleasant Sunday. Clear blue skies and a slight summer breeze set the perfect day for a canoe outing on Lake Mohonk. The lake was nestled in New York State's Shawangunk Mountains. Stryker sat in the rear, paddling, while Leigh sat up front, facing him. She wore a sleeveless white dress, displaying her lithe arms. The tea-length dress fell ten inches below her knees. Even though Stryker couldn't see her knees, he knew what they looked like. They were bony, the way he liked them. She held an aqua-blue parasol to shield her flawless skin from the sun's rays. The blue in the umbrella matched the blue in her eyes. She talked gayly about a number of light topics such as the weather or activities she had planned for them. Stryker responded with short accommodative replies. All during the canoeing, Leigh's radiant smile never left her face. On occasion, she would hang her hand over the side and carelessly drag it in the water.

Above the sloped rocky cliff and overlooking the lake, sat the magnificent Mohonk Mountain House where Stryker and his wife were spending the week. Alfred H. Smiley and his twin brother had purchased the ten-room inn and tavern along with the lake and 300 acres after seeing it in 1869. They turned it into a Victorian castle with fanciful turrets and gabled frames. Using locally quarried stone, workers faced the ground level walls. They also set large rocks boldly and artfully throughout the interior. It boasted 267 guest rooms, most with balconies, 138 fireplaces, and three very large dining rooms. The resort also featured horseback riding, hiking trails, swimming and canoeing in the lake, and a magnificent flower garden stretching over several acres with dazzling beds of tulips–especially tulips–and lilies, daffodils, daisies, roses, rhododendrons, and additional native plants. Several presidents stayed there, along with other notable guests. It was a luxurious resort for a young couple to have an enjoyable holiday.

Stryker could not have ever imagined his good fortune then. He had a good job as one of J.P. Morgan's Vice-Presidents, charged with bringing new defense companies to market in initial public offerings. Leigh's family, the Enderson's, was prominent and well connected, and they'd helped him get the job with the House of Morgan. He worked hard and made Leigh and her family proud.

Leigh was stunningly beautiful, sitting with legs bent at the knees under the parasol and wearing the white dress. With ash-blonde hair and sparkling blue eyes, she looked magazine picturesque with the lake and Sky Top Mountain behind her.

"I am so happy, Neville," Leigh said to him, flashing brilliant teeth in a wide smile. "I hope you can be too." Her smile faded, replaced with a concerned frown.

"I am," he said. Although one never knew with Stryker. He seldom smiled, and he didn't this time either.

Leigh knew that about him and accepted his reply as genuine.

Stryker had paddled out and back the half-mile length of Lake Mohonk, spending the majority of the time staring at Leigh. He asked, "Ready to go in for dinner?"

While lying in jail, he remembered how uncomfortable he was that day, stroking the paddle in a wool, pin-striped suit.

"You must be hungry after all the paddling," Leigh said, and she laughed.

Stryker swung the paddle to the left side of the canoe and angled it toward the dock.

Leigh smiled at Stryker. Yeah, she knew him.

He guided the canoe alongside the pier and one of the attendants helped Leigh step out onto the dock. Stryker waited until she'd gotten her footing on the planks before he hopped out of the canoe. She took his hand and they walked along the pier toward the resort grounds. Adirondack chairs painted red, yellow, and green sat on the lawn under matching-colored umbrellas. Hotel staff wore maroon tuxes with tails and gray pin-striped pants carrying summer drinks on sterling silver trays to guests who relaxed in the chairs. As Leigh and Stryker approached the end of the pier, a man seated in one of the chairs got to his feet and waved. Stryker didn't know the man. He figured Leigh did.

"Miss Enderson," the fellow called out. He was with a group of six people: three couples, including the greeter. The woman seated next to the man also waved. Stryker figured her to be his wife.

"John!" Leigh whispered to Stryker, "Let's stop by and say hello. They were at our wedding."

"Good to see you again, dear," John said. He was a slightly built man with a trimmed mustache and stern countenance. "Please meet my wife, Laura. And this is Andy and his wife, Louise. Andy, who struggled to his feet, was shorter and stouter than John, and he sported a full beard. He also had eyes more kind than John's.

"My husband, Major Neville Stryker. You met at our wedding, John." Leigh reached for Stryker's hand and pulled him forward to stand beside her.

John shook Stryker's hand, and then Andy stepped up to do the same. Stryker judged their grips to be good and strong as if they were men you could depend on. The women remained seated. Stryker thought their wives were what you might call handsome in their own way, but you wouldn't cheat on your wife to be with them. The third couple was not introduced.

"Nice to see you as well, John, Andy." Leigh offered her hand to each of the men. The couple that was not introduced remained seated. Leigh glanced at them, but taking a cue from John, she made no effort to greet them. "This is such a beautiful place here. First time for us." Leigh swiped a hand back and forth indicating she meant her and Stryker.

"Andy must return to New York later today," John began. "Laura and

I will be having breakfast at seven in the morning. Would you and Neville care to join us?"

Leigh glanced at Stryker. He nodded. "Yes, that would be a pleasure."

"Would you prefer the main dining room or the Lakeview Veranda? The main dining room has a better menu," John added.

"The main dining room," Stryker said.

"Good, then we shall see you then."

Stryker took Leigh by the elbow and guided her along the pathway toward the hotel.

"I like him," John told Andy. They returned to sit on their lawn chairs. "He was perceptive enough to know I preferred the main dining room. Smart lad."

"Tonight, after dinner, can we spend a little time listening to music in the parlor?" Leigh asked. "There will be strings, two violins and a cello. Maybe a piano, but I would like to hear the violinists and the cellist. They're from Philadelphia. Would you mind, Stryker?" Leigh beamed a fetching smile and lifted her ash-blonde, slightly curved eyebrows for his answer.

"Like strings myself."

"Good." Leigh stretched high on her feet to kiss Stryker. She couldn't reach his face and he leaned down for the "thank you" peck on his cheek.

After a short rest in their rustic but elegant room, Stryker and Leigh bathed and changed into formal dinner attire. The resort was *mountain casual*; however, the guests were expected to dress up for dinner. The Smileys, being strict Quakers, did not permit drinking on the property, and there was no dancing, but they did encourage dressing up for evening meals in the main dining room. Leigh liked that. Stryker put up with it. Pine wood paneling covered the walls in the main dining room overlooking the lake and the Shawangunk Mountains. It was rustic, but the tables were covered with white tablecloths. He had trouble enjoying the dinner without some kind of alcoholic contribution. Leigh had tea with her freshly caught trout, and Stryker drank black coffee with his steak. Since after-dinner drinks weren't offered, the two of them retired to the parlor for relaxing music instead.

Twenty-eight, plush, velvet-colored, cushioned chairs arranged in semi-circle rows provided guests with comfortable places to sit and listen to the music. The two violinists and one cellist were older men. They wore black tuxedos and sat in straight-back chairs. Smoking, same as drinking, was not allowed in the resort, and every chair afforded listeners a smoke-free view of the musicians. Stryker and Leigh entered the parlor and spied two empty seats by the pine-paneled wall to their left. He led her around the rear row, where he noticed John and Laura were seated.

The trio played a variety of Baroque pieces. Stryker and Leigh listened through two long renditions. Stryker had just about all he could stand (Baroque was not his favorite music) when the first violinist stood and introduced the other two musicians, and then himself. He named the pieces they'd just played and who'd composed them. The audience clapped politely. Stryker hoped the players were about to take a break and then he would suggest a quick exit to Leigh, but that didn't happen.

"Ladies and gentlemen," the violinist continued. "Thank you, thank you so much." He bowed. The other two musicians stood, the violinist and the cellist, and then the three of them bowed together.

"Now I want to say you are in for a real treat," the lead violinist said. The three men remained standing with anticipatory smiles.

"We have in the audience tonight an accomplished and strikingly beautiful violinist. I know this is highly unexpected, but if we could convince her to play tonight, it would grace us all with an unforgettable evening." The speaker gazed out over the audience. "Will you please encourage her with a loud round of applause?" The musicians began applauding and the crowd joined them with boisterous clapping and shouts of encouragement. Audience members, including Stryker, craned their necks in an attempt to identify the mystery musician.

"Miss Enderson, will you please?" The violinist extended an open palm in Leigh's direction. The gesture caused everyone in the parlor to focus their attention on Leigh. No one in the audience except John and Laura, and Stryker, knew *"Miss Enderson."* Obviously, the violinist did not know Leigh was now Mrs. Stryker, but the violinist did know Leigh and that she played the violin as well.

"Neville, is it okay?" Leigh asked, giving him a concerned frown.

"I want to hear you play, Leigh," Stryker assured her.

"I never thought to tell you. Everything happened so fast, I forgot to mention I…," Leigh whispered.

"Go," Stryker interrupted, kissing her on the cheek.

Leigh got up from her chair and headed to the front. Her simple, light blue, Gothic Victorian floor-length gown had white lace covering her bare shoulders, extending to the elbows. The slim, attractive woman cut a strikingly elegant figure walking up the aisle.

When she reached the front, the lead violinist bowed and handed Leigh his instrument. He held his chair for her, and when she sat, he stood by the wall.

Leigh drew the violin under her chin and lifted the bow. She hesitated a moment as if deciding what to play, and then she began. Holding the bow lightly in her thumb and fingers, she flexed her wrist and stroked the bow back and forth, smoothly drawing the rosin across the strings. The fingers on her free hand danced expertly on the strings. With one leg bent and drawn rearward, her back straight and rigid, Leigh swayed gently with the music.

Surprised and proud, Stryker watched his wife play.

The music.

Stryker didn't know the piece. Mellifluous and melancholy. He listened, mesmerized as Leigh played, expressing herself, her mood, with the music. Although she played beautifully, it almost seemed as if each note was painful to play. The violin virtually dripped with sorrow. A chill went through him. His body stiffened. *Why this song? Is there something I don't know?*

When Leigh finished, she stood, laid the violin and bow on the chair, and dipped her head to the audience as they stood and applauded. She returned to sit by Stryker. He noticed she wasn't smiling.

"What was that song?" Stryker whispered.

"*Gnossienne Number One,* by Erik Satie."

"Why did you play it?"

"Not sure, but I suddenly felt an immense sadness, and that song came to me."

"You played well."

"Miss Enderson, take another bow!" The violinist insisted since clapping had not abetted. Leigh stood and dipped her head again, mouthing "thank you." Then she sat. The clapping dwindled as the violinists also took their seats. They resumed playing, and the applause ended alltogether.

Leigh took Stryker's hand in both of hers. She held tightly and he felt her hands tremble twice before she loosened her grip. She didn't let go, though.

He glanced at her and thought he saw fright in her eyes, her face. *From the playing? No, that couldn't be.* He laid his other hand on hers and squeezed to reassure her. The violinists switched to Beethoven's *Moonlight Sonata.* Stryker liked it better, but he had trouble enjoying the music because he sensed something was wrong with Leigh. As he searched his mind for hints he may have missed, he tried to recall anything that might have happened during their short marriage or prior to that. Their life together seemed perfect. He might have said she was almost perfect, but he couldn't think of a flaw. He could not recall her ever losing her temper, raising her voice in anger, or making disparaging remarks about anybody. She often deferred to him and did so while offering logical opinions, which sometimes prevented him from making a fool of himself. He couldn't ask more from a woman. There was a goodness about her, and she was a radiant beauty now in her mid-twenties. But he'd still adore her after she aged. Leigh would always be beautiful to Stryker.

Later in the privacy of their room, they spent the night making love. Stryker, more experienced in conjugation, gently guided Leigh, helping her to enjoy herself. The girl had only been with Stryker, but she'd heard stories about how it was supposed to be. Achieving simultaneous orgasms for instance, naively thinking that was what it was all about, not knowing there was much more to sexual delight. As their time together grew, he would try to give Leigh as much pleasure as he could, but that would wait. She was young and not ready to freely communicate her desires. She was too shy now. In the future, Stryker would find out what pleased her. He'd learned early on the best sex was finding out what a woman liked and doing it for her. Often, she never knew what she liked before trying new things, and only then would she realize what lit her fire. He would make Leigh comfortable with him so she would feel free to explore. Stryker wanted to give her great pleasure because he loved her. For tonight, they achieved orgasms together and that made her happy.

The following morning, they met John and Laura in the main dining room for breakfast. They spent three hours together, discussing a wide range of topics, including politics, business, religion, and philanthropy. John was a Northern Baptist who read the Bible daily and tithed ten percent of his income.

"We like this place, Stryker." John looked around the room as he spoke. "We come here often because there is no gambling, no drinking, no smoking, and it is a wonderful place for Laura and me to relax."

"I think we'll return here as well," Leigh said. "Although, I don't think it's because they don't have alcohol!"

"I know," said John. "Not many feel the way I do. I don't believe in prohibition, though. There would be too much corruption." Turning to Stryker he changed the subject. "You were a major in the Army, and now I understand you work for J.P. Morgan, bringing munitions companies to market," John said, cutting into a piece of ham. He pinned it with his fork and stuck it in his mouth.

"That's right."

"I think you'll do just fine there, but if you ever tire of it, you can always work for me. I'm a pretty good judge of character."

"Thanks, John," Stryker replied, hovering his knife and fork over his steak and eggs.

"You played beautifully last night," Laura said to Leigh. "John and I both commented on your virtuosity and the song. What song was that?"

"*Gnossienne Number One.*"

"Don't believe we've heard it before." Laura glanced at John who shook his head.

"By Satie." Leigh smiled politely. "It's a new one by him."

"At one time, I thought I might pursue music," John said. "After high school, I took a ten-week bookkeeping course instead. Probably better for it," he laughed. "Well, you two, I have a Sunday School class to teach." John signaled for the waiter. When the waiter approached, he had the man bend down and whispered, "Put the meals on my check."

Stryker heard and started to protest.

Leigh gripped Stryker by the arm and leaned closer. "Don't make a scene, Neville."

John and Laura stood. "So glad to have had breakfast with you," Laura said. And John added with a sly grin to Stryker, "Remember what I said about you tiring of J.P." They walked from the dining room and the Strykers never had the occasion to meet them again.

John and Laura Rockefeller visited the Mohonk Mountain House. *Andy* may not have been there with them at the time of meeting the Strykers, but Andrew Carnegie and John D. Rockefeller did do deals together. Andrew's wife, whom he had married in 1887, was named Louise. John D. Rockefeller was widely regarded as the richest man in America. At the time he was worth close to one billion dollars (in 1888 dollars), roughly 3% of the U.S. GDP. Before Rockefeller, kerosene lamps were produced with a wide variety of mixtures, so much so, that people burned their houses down because the lamps often exploded. He standardized kerosene production and made it cheap enough for the average home-owner to buy. It was the beginning of Standard Oil. The company grew to 20,000 oil wells, 4,000 miles of pipeline, 5,000 tank cars, 100,000 employees, and it produced 90% of the world's oil. In 1911, the company was broken up into thirty different companies, including Exxon, Mobile, Chevron, Esso, and Sohio. The Rockefeller family's wealth today is in excess of $360 billion. John and Andrew gave away enough of their wealth to be generally thought of as the fathers of structured philan-thropy. Not bad for a man who never went to college or studied geology.

Stryker and Leigh remained at the breakfast table. "Did you ever figure out what was bothering you last night?" he asked her.

"No, just a foreboding feeling of something. Probably nothing really. Let's forget about it." Leigh reached for his hand and squeezed it.

Was it something she feared would happen? Can I prevent it?

CHAPTER EIGHT

Something did happen and he didn't prevent it. Stryker escaped the memory and resumed his stay in the Denver jail. Leigh was dead, and he had a hand in her death. He should have re-checked the coordinates on the damn guns. Leigh lay dying that day because he hadn't done his job. He was too eager to impress by using new indirect artillery fire, he failed her. She died in his arms.

His name–even then she hadn't said his name in anger.

He killed the man who switched the firing coordinates, a competitor, but all that did was get revenge out of the way to make more room for guilt and grief. Emotions still weighed heavily on him, and if he managed to get them out of his head during the day, he had nightmares of finding Leigh's body shattered and broken, bloodied, and blackened with gunpowder. Even after all the years, Stryker remained a remorseful, angry, and wretched man.

He is a very dangerous man to cross. Stryker is a ruthless killer. No one gets a second chance. A man who is not afraid to die, and survives with animal instinct is a terrible foe; he's a man best left alone.

"I've had a bad week."

Stryker recognized the girl's voice. It came from the cell next to him. He must have dozed and didn't hear them bring her in, not like him. His sixth sense had failed to alert him. *Must be slipping*. Stryker knew that wasn't the case, though. He was absorbed with his memory of Leigh. He sat up and swung his feet to the floor. It was late at night and there was little light in the cell section. Ambient light from a crescent moon came through the cell window, but it was not enough for Stryker to see her face. He remained sitting on the cot. "Raelyn."

"My husband's dead, and I'm in jail." Raelyn bumped into her own cot and plopped down. "They guessed you weren't my cousin and wanted to know who the hell you were. I told them I had no idea. Shit, you really could be my cousin for all I know." Raelyn sobbed.

The girl has had a bad time of it. "I'll get us out of here," Stryker said. He wasn't sure how. He still had the sai and a razor, but if he broke out, they'd be on the run. That would make it difficult to see Smith and find the painting. However, being at the end of a rope would make it impossible. One thing though, the police were on Smith's payroll. That means they could be bribed, and the Mackeys had money. It could be a bit tricky.

"Jailor!" Stryker yelled. "I want a lawyer!"

Of course, the police were bribed, and they delivered to the highest bidder. The lawyer was well-paid as well, and he kept his mouth shut for a second payment. Witnesses turned up who claimed they saw Max and Mable assault Stryker and that Stryker had acted in self-defense. The witness's testimony was corroborated when Zeke was compelled to take off his shirt and show the knife wound. The case was dismissed. The district attorney was paid off, too. Soapy had money, but he couldn't match a rich miner's millions. The details of the maneuverings were unsavory, despicable, and effective.

. . .

"Stryker, you and Miss Raelyn are free to go," Bill the sheriff, said. "Ride out of here tonight, and don't come back. It's half-past midnight." He unlocked the cell door and held it open for Stryker to walk out.

"Here's your gun." He handed the gun belt with the holstered Colt to Stryker. "Soapy ain't gonna like you gettn' outta jail, but there's nothing I can do about it. Witnesses swore 'fore Judge Claiborne you was innocent. Humpf!" Bill grunted his disapproval. "I don't believe 'em but the law says to let you go. Get the hell of town tonight, Stryker. Be long gone before Soapy finds out." Bill slammed the cell door shut.

The Sheriff stepped to Raelyn's cell door and unlocked it. "Don't know how you're mixed up in this, but you can go too." He gripped her upper arm. "Miss, if you want my advice, get on the train and leave town. Get away from him." Bill nodded toward Stryker. "And get away from Soapy, too. Neither one good for a girl like you. That's all." He released her and went about locking the two cell doors. "Might not go so easily next time," he mumbled to himself. Neither Stryker nor Raelyn heard him. They were walking out the front door.

"I want your help again," Stryker said. Raelyn had started at a brisk pace down the sidewalk when Stryker caught up with her. He spun her around. "Where were you headed?"

"Taking the Sheriff's advice. To the train station."

Raelyn turned away and started off again.

Stryker called after her, "You have money?"

She stopped suddenly, brought her feet together, and slowly turned back to Stryker. He stood ten feet away, and in the cloudy moonlight, he was all but a tall shadowy figure to her now. "No, I don't." She admitted, sounding surprised by the revelation.

"Do it. I'll buy your train fare."

"What if you're dead. How you gonna do that?" Raelyn remained standing in place. "And me, what about me? Killings follow you, Stryker. I don't wanna be another one."

The girl has a point. "Take twenty minutes."

"What," Raelyn huffed. "What'll I have to do?"

"Walk back to Tivoli's. Go in the front door and up to Soapy's office.

If he's by himself, close the door behind you. Give him a hug and knock on the rear door once. I'll be by the door."

"If he's not alone, then what?"

"Tell him about the painting, and I'll pay a lot of money for it."

"That's it?"

"That's it."

"Okay."

Stryker and Raelyn walked together until they were a block away from the saloon. There Raelyn stopped. "Where will we meet afterward, for you to give me the money?"

Stryker dug in his front pocket and pulled out a wad of twenty-dollar bank notes. He peeled off two of the brown backs and handed them to her.

She grabbed the notes and quickly stuffed them down the front of her dress. "You trust me, I guess," she said.

"I wouldn't want to kill you."

"God, Stryker! I think you mean it."

Even with faint light, Stryker saw the fright on her face. "Go. I'll be by the back door," he ordered.

Although it was after midnight, saloons and gambling halls in Denver were busy. Whether the patrons were out-of-town miners, cattle drovers, or locals out for drinking and gambling, tonight, as usual, the Tivoli saloon was crowded and noisy. Stryker made his way down the alleyway, and Raelyn watched him disappear in the darkness before finally deciding to turn and walk the rest of the way to the Tivoli saloon.

Raelyn pushed through the front doors. It was late enough for the men to have more than a drink or two in them. Loud and boisterous, they were having a good time. The band was still playing, but the music was drowned out by hooting and hollering. Tobacco smoke wafted about and was thick enough to cut with a knife. Saloon girls whirled around the floor with men who bought dances for a dollar. Other women hung around card players soliciting drinks for luck, or from bar drinkers for companionship. Soapy wouldn't let the women drink alcohol, though. They drank tea instead. Four guards stationed along the walls watched the women entertain the men to make sure things didn't get out of hand.

Occasionally, one of the girls, a prostitute, would accompany a yearning fellow arm in arm up the stairs for a short tryst in one of the crib rooms. Raelyn fell in behind a couple and headed up the stairs with them. Threesomes were rare, but they did happen, and Raelyn reached the second floor unnoticed by the guards.

Upstairs was just as noisy as the saloon downstairs, even more, made so by gamblers yelling as dealers threw dice on *Grand Hazard* tables. Raelyn walked straight up to a guard and said, "Soapy sent for me. He said to tell you not to interrupt us. Guess you know what that means." The guard hesitated a moment, gave Raelyn a shit-eating grin, and then nodded toward the office.

Soapy sat in the office alone behind his desk. She closed the door and ran around the desk to hug him. She'd startled Soapy, but he enjoyed the hugging. "Thank you for getting me out of jail, Soapy!" Raelyn *accidentally* kicked the rear door with her heel.

Stryker pulled the razor and eased the door open. Raelyn had kept her word. Just she and Soapy were in the office. Raelyn had her arms wrapped around his neck, and she was slathering wet kisses all around his bearded face.

Stryker grasped the back of the girl's collar and ripped backward, almost dragging the saloon owner out of his chair before she let go of his neck. The mixed breed cupped his hand under Soapy's chin and jerked upward. Stryker placed the razor under the scraggily beard and dug in the tip. Blood oozed from the cut and made a crimson rivulet down Soapy's throat.

"Don't move," Stryker growled.

"What you want?" Soapy squeaked.

"Don't kill him, Stryker!" Raelyn yelled louder than she meant to.

"Where's the Yellow House painting?" Stryker wasn't fucking around.

Soapy knew it. "I sold it."

Stryker dug the razor deeper.

"I sold it to Al, Alex Rooney!" Soapy's voice rose another octave. "He's got a cattle ranch west of Denver." He talked fast, trying to beat the razor.

"Prove it," Stryker said.

"Prove… I don't know how… wait!" Soapy tried to turn around and the blade stopped him. "I have a receipt, a sales receipt in there." He pointed toward the second desk drawer. "I'll get it for you."

"You won't live long enough to pull out a gun." Stryker kept the razor on Soapy's throat and used his free hand to push the man's shoulders toward the drawer.

"It's in the 'Art' file." Smith eased the drawer open and reached inside the first hanging file. He pulled the file out to lay on his desk, and Stryker eased up with the blade. "It's in here." Smith sifted through several handwritten receipts before he found the one titled "Yellow House." Soapy said, "Hold the lantern closer so Stryker can read it, Raelyn."

The sales slip written to Alexander Rooney referenced "The Yellow House" painting was sold to him for $150.

"Where's the ranch?" Stryker picked up the receipt.

"Get on the road due west out of Denver." Soapy cleared his throat. "Can you take the knife off my neck?" He didn't know it was a razor.

"Then what." Stryker pulled the razor away from Soapy's neck and rested the dripping blade on the gambler's shoulders.

Soapy's voice gained a little confidence. "The ranch is between Green Mountain and Hogback Ridge. It's a stone ranch house. You'll see the cattle. Al runs ten-thousand head out there."

Stryker stepped from Smith and backed toward the door. "What are you doing here?" he asked Raelyn.

It took a moment for her to realize why Stryker asked the question. "I came to thank Soapy for getting me out of jail."

Stryker spun and slipped out the back door.

"You're bleeding, Soapy." Raelyn said, as she went around the desk and picked up a towel off the cot. "Here, let me clean it off you." She dabbed the towel down Soapy's neck, and then moistened the towel with her mouth to wipe away as much blood as she could from his shirt collar.

"He was… about to kill me," Soapy squeaked. He cleared his throat. "I've never been that close to death." He felt his neck. Taking his hand away, he saw he was still bleeding.

"He's a killer, Soapy. I've seen him kill four just this past week. Maybe he won't come back."

"How the hell did he get outta jail? Say, how'd you get out?"

"I don't know." Raelyn didn't know how Stryker had arranged their releases. "I thought you got me out," she lied.

"No, but I was going too. I shouldn't have had you locked up. I think you saved my life tonight."

"Soapy, I'm planning to leave town. I want to go back east, back home." Raelyn draped the bloody towel over the cot rail. "I don't think the violence out here in the west is for me. I want to go to New York, even if I gotta work my way to get there." She turned to face him. She dropped her arms to her sides. "Please, will you pay me what you owe me for the three nights I worked?"

Soapy slid a drawer open. He counted out fifteen dollars. He laid them on the edge of the desk. "You can make a lot more here if you want." Soapy cocked his head with raised eyebrows.

"No, not that way. Besides I just want to go home." Raelyn walked to the door. "Goodbye, Soapy." She walked out, leaving the door open.

Raelyn crossed the gambling hall floor, went downstairs, and exited Tivoli's. Without looking back, she made her way to the train station and bought the next ticket east. It was scheduled for four hours later, and she waited. She never saw Soapy again. Jefferson "Soapy" Smith was run out of Denver a short time later, and he traveled to Alaska where he resumed playing his scams until someone shot and killed him. Raelyn did make it to New York and never saw the mixed breed again.

Stryker headed for the roan. It might have been an hour, maybe two after midnight, he didn't know, and it didn't matter. He passed more saloons and things hadn't quieted down yet. The drinking and hollering usually abated when the sun came up. The night grew colder and he quickened his pace. Along the boardwalk, Stryker thought about why he hadn't cut Smith's throat. Soapy sure deserved it. There was a slight chance he might need him alive later, so there was that. Also, maybe Soapy owed Raelyn money. It was one of the few times a man crossed Stryker and lived. He also figured he could kill him later.

Stryker entered the Windsor Hotel to pick up a shirt, shave kit, and the coat he'd left in the room. It was quiet in the lobby except for two clerks behind the counter, talking about who got whipped more as a kid. Stryker walked through the lobby and climbed the stairs to his room. Passing the second floor, a few men were losing their money in the gambling hall, but they weren't as noisy as regular saloons. There were better-behaved guests at the hotel. A few minutes later, he came back downstairs with his carry bag. He wore the coat. The clerks still hadn't settled the argument about the whippings.

He didn't see an attendant in the hotel stable. Not wanting to wait until daylight, Stryker found the roan, put on the bridle and bit, and saddled it himself. The .44-40 still hung in the boot. He tied on the bedroll, a wool blanket in a canvas tarp, behind the saddle. A half bag of oats lay in a saddle bag. Two pieces of hardtack, three slices of salted pork, and canned coffee grounds were in the other bag; they were provisions he had left over from the last trail ride. Would have to do for the night's ride. He briefly mused he would have gotten a hot breakfast in jail–but then hanged later.

Clouds had thinned and with a three-quarter moon, Stryker was able to pick up the well-traveled trail leading west out of Denver. He'd started at an easy canter and then allowed the horse to walk once getting out of sight from the last building. Roughly five miles out of town, he reined the roan off the road and let it pick its own way along a stream up a meadow. Rocky slopes scaled up to heavily forested blue-tip spruce and ponderosa pines on both sides. After another half mile up the meadow, he halted the roan and dismounted. It wasn't the Windsor Hotel, but he wanted two or three hours of sleep before he rode on to the Rooney ranch. Not knowing what kind of reception he'd receive once he got there, he needed to be ready. He took off the roan's bit and bridle and put on the halter. After pulling the saddle, he used a lead line to the halter to stake out the horse. He threw a few oats on the ground for the roan to eat. Afterward, it could graze in the lush grass next to the creek. He picked out a thick patch of grass and laid out the bedroll. Taking off the gun belt and his boots, Stryker wrapped himself in the blanket to catch a little sleep. One might think a good warm bed would provide him the best sleep, but a bedroll out in the open on a clear night suited the mixed breed better. He woke just as the sky was beginning to gray.

He built a cooking fire using pine needles and branches he found lying under the trees. After setting two rocks in the fire to use as a crude grate, he filled the coffee pot from the creek, added grounds, and set it on the rocks. It took twenty minutes for the water to boil. Then he tipped the pot and poured coffee into his cup. Steam rose from the cup, and he sipped it trying not to burn his mouth. The coffee tasted strong and hot. He held the tin cup in his hands for a short while before taking another sip. Then he bit into the hard tack and pork and the tough crust scraped the roof of his mouth. He dunked the biscuit in the coffee to soften it.

It grew lighter, and the hills on both sides of the meadow began to take shape. The hills weren't all that high, but the foothills warned travelers the soaring Rockies lay not much farther to the west. He couldn't yet see the massive mountains rising over fourteen thousand feet, but they were there just past the hills, waiting for travelers who dared challenge them. He finished the coffee, thinking he was glad he didn't have to ride a horse across the Rockies to San Francisco. He figured the roan would feel that way too. After he got the painting, he'd go to a train depot and buy the tickets to San Francisco. He may not see Mrs. Mackey again, but that was fine with him. It was most likely fine with the woman as well.

Time to get the artwork.

Stryker rinsed the cup and coffee pot in the creek. He picked up the canteen, emptied it on the fire, and refilled it. It took him twenty minutes to saddle the roan. The trail returning to the road turned out to be a cattle trail used for bringing a herd to the meadow and back. He hadn't noticed the cow pies in the dark. Once he'd ridden back to the road, and gone about a mile, he spotted a small herd of cattle. He counted six cowboys working them in a narrow grassy valley about a half mile from him. Stryker didn't figure on running into Rooney cattle this far out from the ranch, but the rancher had a big herd. He reined the roan off the road and goaded it toward the cattle.

As Stryker got closer, he saw three cowboys branding cows by an open campfire. The remaining three men tended the herd while the branding was being done. The smell of singed hide and hair infiltrated his nostrils, but it wasn't until he got within a few feet of the branding that he realized the men weren't just punching cattle. They were *re-branding* cattle, turning Rs into Bs. *Cattle Rustlers.*

They hadn't noticed him ride up, or so he thought. Stryker reined the roan around and saw one of the cowboys tending herd, had ridden up behind him. The loud mooing drowned out his approach. *Shit,* Stryker cursed himself for paying too much attention to the re-branding. The rustler had a carbine pointed at Stryker and looked eager to use it.

"Hey, Buck!" The rustler shouted. "We got company!"

The branding trio leaped to their feet, drawing pistols. "Who are you, mister? What you want?"

Stryker swung the roan around to the branding fire. He figured the man asking questions was Buck. The top rustler was a stout man at just under six-feet. He had a week-old beard and fiercely stern countenance. It was easy to see why he was the leader.

"Asked you a question," Buck growled, walking toward Stryker. He'd asked two questions, but no one was counting. Buck thumbed back the hammer on a Navy Colt.

Stryker reasoned it wasn't the time to say he was looking for Al Rooney. "Looking for a job."

"Ain't hiring."

The other two cowboys doing the branding stepped around the fire with cocked pistols, and joined Buck. Rustling cattle was a hanging crime in the 1880s. Killing a nosy stranger might keep ropes coiled on saddles, and not around their necks.

"Don't shoot him yet," Buck ordered. "Mister, unbuckle your gun belt with your left hand. Do it real slow-like, and drop it on the ground." Buck canted his head toward the rustler standing closest to him, but he kept his eyes on Stryker. "Take his carbine out too, Tupo. Careful now, I don't like his looks."

Buck stepped closer to the roan. "Hold it, Tupo. Give your gun to me first."

Tupo, a small wiry man missing an arm, suddenly stopped two steps in front of the roan as if he'd been lassoed. He handed his pistol to Buck. Tupo, carefully eyeing Stryker, said, "Don't try nothin', mister." He moved up and slid the Winchester from its scabbard.

"Now you and Hen tie him up. Hen, hand me your gun too," Buck ordered. Hen un-cocked his pistol's hammer and gave it to Buck. "You still got two guns on you, mister." Buck stuck Hen's gun in his waistband.

Stryker figured the only reason they didn't kill him right away was to keep from spooking the cattle.

"Don't care who I work for. Just need enough to get to San Francisco. Couple days here ought to do it," Stryker drawled. He leaned forward, resting his forearms on the saddle horn. "I got in a little trouble back east, and I got a woman in California I wanna see again."

Sure, Stryker lied. He figured he was going to hell anyway. Telling the truth right now would get him there a lot quicker though.

"What you wanted for?" Buck grunted.

"Killed a man."

"Pull 'im off and tie him up." Buck eased the hammer forward, but he waited until Stryker was seated on the ground with arms and legs tied before he holstered the Colt. The two rustlers who tied Stryker used the lariat on the roan. Buck walked over to the sitting mixed breed and looked down on Stryker. "We'll decide what to do wit' you later."

"Shoot me or hire me. Don't like being tied," Stryker growled.

You could tell Buck was wrestling with both ideas. "Let's get back to the brandin' boys." The three of them strode back to the branding fire, and Stryker could hear them talking about what to do about him. Hen roped a calf and wrestled it over to the fire. Buck pulled the iron from the fire and rammed it home on the R. The bawling calf drowned out their talking. The rustler cowboy who'd come up behind him swung his horse around and returned to the herd.

Tupo, using one arm, was having a rough time wrestling a calf past Stryker to the fire. He had a rope on the calf but it was in no mood to approach the branding. Other calves made loud and painful bawling after the branding, and the critter didn't want any part of what caused their anguish.

"Lose it in the war?" Stryker asked. There were a lot of amputees after the Civil War. One in every seven men in Mississippi had lost a limb.

"Yeah, Goddammit!" Tupo wasn't having much success with the calf. He'd pull it a few feet toward the fire and then it would splay its legs and jerk back, causing Tupo to lose his grip on the rope. He'd tried looping the rope around his hand and almost lost another arm.

Stryker began to suspect this *was* their first rodeo. Watching the somewhat comical battle, he managed to maneuver a hand into his back pocket and work out the razor. He started cutting the rope. The rustlers failed to notice Stryker freeing himself.

"Need a hand, Tupo?" Stryker knelt beside the calf, weighing roughly a hundred-fifty pounds, slid his arms under it, and raised up.

Tupo tripped over a rock and almost fell, stepping away from Stryker with the calf. "Whoa! Hey! How'd you…?"

Stryker carried the calf to the branding fire and set it down with his knee on its neck. Tupo followed. He stood behind the kneeling mixed breed. At first Buck and Hen, busy branding a calf, failed to see it was Stryker who'd brought another one over. Buck released the bawling calf and Hen turned to stick the branding iron in the fire. It was then he glanced over to the next calf and saw Stryker.

"Buck," Hen said, "that fellow got loose."

"What the fuck? Where'd he go?" Buck cursed, swinging around to find Stryker holding down the calf next to him.

"You men aren't much good at rustling," Stryker said. "I'm not either, but we better hurry up and move these cows out of here before someone else comes down that road."

Buck and Stryker locked eyes and then Buck grunted, "Hit the iron on it, Hen."

Hen jammed the glowing B on the R. "He's right, Buck. I guess we better get this beef to Denver."

"Hen, help Tupo bring me anothern'," Buck ordered, turning to Stryker. "What's your name, mister?"

"Stryker."

"Why'd you kill 'im?"

Stryker pondered telling the truth, but the idea of it reminded him of his own role in his wife's death. "Asked too many questions."

"We only got forty head here. Ain't much profit divided six ways, much less seven," Buck said, watching Tupo and Hen wrestle with a cow.

"What you figure to get for them in Denver?"

"I'd say, $20 for the full grown, maybe $2.50 for the calves. Total around uh…"

"One thousand two hundred twenty-five dollars." Stryker had already counted out the small herd–30 cows, 10 calves, no bulls–and being in the artillery, he was good with math. "A little over two hundred dollars each for six men."

"Ye-ah," Buck stuttered.

Stryker figured Buck's hesitancy meant things weren't quite equal–or Buck was lousy in arithmetic.

"What's seven do?" Buck asked.

"One hundred seventy-five dollars, if divided equally." Stryker guessed Buck probably got more, though.

"I reckon we don't need another man, Stryker."

"All right."

"Stryker, as you can see, we ain't much on the rustling business," Buck said. "After the war, we had it rough. We lost our help, black and white, and the crops rotted in the fields. Then the carpetbaggers came down from the north and swindled us out of our land. Me and the boys are flat broke. We got families to feed back home." He turned to Hen. "Put it in the fire, Hen!" The B on Hen's branding iron had gone from red to black.

"Where you boys from?" Stryker asked.

"The three out there on the herd, Dave, Russ, and Taylor are from Georgia. Tupo's from Mississippi, Tupelo. Why we call him Tupo. And

Henry, or Hen is from Tennessee. I'm from Mississippi too. We All met during the war."

"Good luck with the cows." Stryker spun on his heels and headed over to retrieve the six-shooter and carbine. Both still lay on the ground. He half-expected a bullet in the back, but it didn't happen. *Maybe Buck draws a line between cattle rustling and shooting a man in the back.* He picked up the Peacemaker first and holstered it. He grabbed the Winchester off the ground and walked over to the roan to mount. That's when he heard Buck arguing with Tupo and Hen. Stryker couldn't hear what they were saying but figured it had something to do with his leaving. They got louder.

Stryker!" Buck shouted. "We can't let you just ride outta here." Hen and Tupo moved up to stand beside Buck.

Stryker squared himself to the three men and brought the front stock of carbine up to cradle in his left hand. They had yet to draw guns. Dave, and the other two men guarding the cattle, Russ and Taylor were at least forty yards away. Riding herd, they hadn't caught on to the standoff.

Cows closest to Stryker and the three men facing him stopped chewing their cuds and watched what was about to happen. Calves suckling on them paid no attention.

"We've agreed you need to stay…" Buck didn't get to finish.

Another man might have let him finish telling Stryker what the three men decided. Another man might have let them make the first move. Another man might have tried to talk things over or try to diffuse things.

Stryker is not one of those men. He brought the Winchester to bear and shot Hen and Buck before they could draw. Red splashes appeared around the black bullet holes in their shirts, and the two men toppled to the ground. Stryker drew a bead on Tupo who held up an empty hand, as if to surrender. The .44 slug smashed him in the chest, left of center. Stryker swung the Winchester rearward. The front line of cattle pushed away from the gunfire. Oddly though, they made no sound, and they didn't run. Perhaps the simple beasts somehow sensed the shooting was meant for the three rustlers on the ground.

The shots alerted the rustlers riding herd. After watching their buddies fall, they swung their horses around and took off at a hard gallop. Stryker sighted in on Taylor who was the slowest rider but then relaxed. He lifted his face off the Winchester and watched the cowboys get to the road, where they turned left toward Denver. Stryker shoved the carbine in the scabbard and mounted the roan.

Stealing cattle had not worked out for the cowboys today. Many would question the actions of Stryker, callously killing those three rustlers the way he did, perhaps justifiably so. But he carried no regrets as he rode away. He had no regrets about shooting the cattle thieves anyway. He had plenty of other regrets, though. One giant one concerning Leigh's death. It was a heavy load. And as time went on, he'd probably gather more to put in his saddlebags or on his shoulders, where he carried Leigh. Nevertheless, the men on the ground had crossed him, and the mixed breed was a dangerous man to cross. Those who do, don't get a second chance. The cattle settled down. Cows munched grass. Calves suckled udders. Except for the three rustlers who lay dead in the grass, life went on.

The sun climbed higher in the blue sky now and Stryker felt its heat through the denim jacket he wore. After riding a half mile to the road, he guided the roan west. The fescue-covered ground spread out for miles north and south. If Stryker had ridden here a few decades ago, he might have seen large herds of buffalo, but the beasts had been heavily slaughtered; their numbers were greatly reduced by the 1880s. Ahead of him, maybe another four or five miles, he saw a long hill running across the horizon. It was a drumlin formation, formed long ago by glaciers. On its higher elevations, ponderosa pines grew, and they were especially thick on the northern slope. The road curved up through a saddle in the hill, and past it followed more hills. Continuing west, they grew bigger until they became the towering Rockies. Roughly five more miles on the road, he heard the cattle before he saw them. Then the enormous herd came into view after he crested the saddle. He figured the rustlers stole the forty head of cattle from this herd, most likely during the night before. The sea of living beef spanned the horizon. More distant cattle disappeared in a huge dust cloud. Cacophonous cattle moos, wrangler shouts, and whistles rose with the dust. Stryker counted at least twenty mounted cowboys riding herd, and he was sure there were more he couldn't see. The enormous herd of cattle was quite a sight. They straddled the road, and Stryker would have to ride around an extra quarter mile to get around them. He got closer and saw the R brand on their hides.

Stryker reined the roan toward the nearest cowboy. When he got within a few feet of him, he shouted, "Looking for a man named Rooney!"

The cowboy wore a dusty Cattleman crease hat, a red bandana over his face, a sweat-stained shirt, and a pair of well-worn chaps over his denims. "What you want wit' 'im?" He shouted back through the bandana.

"Like to buy something from him."

"Beef?"

"No, a painting," Stryker yelled, bringing the roan close enough so they didn't have to yell, yell as loud anyway. Dust was caking up on his teeth and when he ran his tongue over them, he tasted dirt and cow shit. He drew up his handkerchief over his mouth and nose.

"A what?"

"A painting, artwork." Stryker started to feel awkward, realizing he surely did not appear to be, nor did he want to be mistaken for, a fancy-pants art connoisseur. "He has a damn painting my client wants back!"

The cowboy pointed at two men, one astride a bay, and the other on a chestnut. They were higher up the hill and maybe two-hundred feet away from the cattle. One of the men was pointing at something in the herd as they surveyed the cattle.

"That's him with the trail boss up there," the cowboy shouted.

Stryker spurred the roan's flanks and the horse started up the hill at a cantor. He brought it to a walk twenty paces from the two men. The rider on the chestnut looked the better dresser, and Stryker pulled up next to him.

"Alexander Rooney," Stryker called out the man's full name.

"That's me. What can I do for you?" Rooney, who appeared well over six feet, even sitting on a horse. He was dusty too, as much as the other wranglers, but the dust hung on better clothing. A leather tooled vest, ingrained colorful chaps, and the chestnut was a fine-looking animal. Sitting ramrod straight on the horse, he had a deeply tanned, craggy face, and a square jaw. His hazel eyes peered intensely beneath bushy eyebrows. A few white hairs peppered the brows. "You looking for work, son?"

Stryker never liked that "son" appellation, for himself or others. To him, it meant anyone called a son was deemed inferior, naïve, and lacking in manhood. It was only by the strength of purpose he didn't draw the Peacemaker and teach Rooney a lesson in nomenclature. Instead, he growled with an even more fearsome countenance than usual–if that were indeed possible. "Name's Stryker."

Rooney shot a glance to his cattle foreman, and then back to the mixed breed. "What's on your mind, Stryker?" Rooney shifted uncomfortably in his saddle.

"Two things. There's forty head of your cattle five miles east of here, half a mile off the road," Stryker said. "Saw six men switching brands. Three are dead. Three ran off."

"You shoot 'em?" The trail boss asked, scrunching the bushy brows into an angry scowl.

"Yes."

"Now you figure I owe you something," Rooney said flatly.

Stryker allowed that to pass without comment.

"All right then. I reckon that's the second thing. How much?"

"Keep your money. I want the painting you bought from Soapy Smith."

"A painting?" Rooney straightened in the saddle. "You want a painting for saving my cattle?"

"Got a yellow house in the picture. You paid one hundred fifty dollars. I'll give you two hundred for it."

"What's so special about this painting, Stryker?" Rooney asked. You could tell he was curious.

"It was stolen. The owner wants it back. They hired me to get it, one way or another." The threat was obvious.

"All right, Stryker. You did me right. You can have it for the $150 I paid. Go on up to the ranch house and give my wife the money. Tell her I said to sell it to you for that price. You got the cash on you?" Without waiting for an answer, and without taking his eyes off Stryker, he said. "Go with him, Stoney. Then come right back."

"You have the money, Stryker?" Stoney asked. He was a shorter man, maybe five-ten, and a wiry hundred and fifty pounds. Stoney appeared older than he was. The weathered face was from being out in the western sun for much of his thirty-five years, and it added at least ten more. He looked like a man who took his job seriously, a no-nonsense trail boss.

Stryker pulled a wad of U.S. currency notes from his front pocket and held it out for the two men to see.

"Be back in an hour, boss." Stoney swung the bay around and spurred it into a fast trot.

Stryker stuffed the bills in his pocket and heeled the roan to a cantor to catch up with Stoney.

They'd ridden side by side in silence for a mile when Stoney asked, "Why'd you shoot 'em?"

"I wanted the painting."

"What does the painting have to do with it?"

"Figured Rooney would be grateful."

"You kill three men thinkin' Al would give you the painting?"

Stryker said nothing.

Stryker and Stoney rode with no more talking until a mile and a half later when the ranch house came into view. Not a particularly elegant mansion for a cattle baron. At thirty-six by twenty-four feet, the two-story dwelling with windows front and back on each floor was built with cut stone. The rear abutted against a steep hill dotted with juniper pines. A spring house on the left side of the house provided cool storage for milk and butter. Two mature Gambel oaks stood in the front yard, right and left of the house. They had to be the sturdy kind to survive at six-thousand feet altitude and infrequent rainfall in the summer. The two men rode up to the front, dismounted, and tied the horses to a hitching post. Stoney went to the front door near the right corner and knocked.

There was no response. "Mrs. Rooney, it's me, Stoney! She's not gonna answer unless she knows who it is," Stoney whispered to Stryker.

The door cracked open and then drew wider. "Stoney! Has something happened to Alex?" Mrs. Rooney's intelligent eyes and sharp features made her look the part of a schoolteacher, which she was. Not skinny, and certainly not fat, she held herself well, wearing a white long sleeve blouse and denim kitchen apron over a tan ankle-length skirt. Her smile disappeared in a hurry.

"No ma'am," Stoney said, taking off his hat. "He sent me here with Mister Stryker." He hooked a thumb over his shoulder.

"Al's selling him a painting ya'll have."

Mrs. Rooney peeked around Stoney to see Stryker and recoiled back from the doorway.

"It's all right, Mrs Rooney. Apparently, the art was stolen, and Mister Stryker would like to buy it back for the rightful owner."

Stryker thought Stoney explained his mission well enough and added, "Mean no harm, ma'am."

"Please come in." Mrs. Rooney threw open the door. As Stryker brushed passed by her, he doffed the Stetson. She studied the tall man's features more closely, and upon closing the door, she said, "Please sit down. Would you like some coffee? I just made some." Without receiving an answer, she marched into the kitchen.

Both men stopped in the middle of the room, looked around the furnishings, and sat. Stoney plopped down on a green, quilt-covered settee, Stryker sat on a straight-back chair with slats. Stoney glanced at Stryker and gave him a nod, which the mixed breed didn't acknowledge. While waiting for Mrs. Rooney to bring coffee, Stryker glanced around the room. It wasn't very large, but it was a comfortable parlor for receiving guests. Stairs a few steps from the front door ran up along the wall which led to a second floor. An oak coffee table by the settee, an over-stuffed chair with a lamp stand, and two more wooden chairs like Stryker's, made up the furniture. Kerosene lamps on the rough-stoned walls provided additional light during the evenings, or on cloudy days. Hot apple pie's sweet aroma wafted from the kitchen.

"Don't get up," Mrs. Rooney said, coming into the room with three mugs of coffee and two slices of the pie on a silver tray. "Alex brought the painting home four days ago. He said he wanted to build a new house like it." She offered the pie and coffee to Stryker, and then to Stoney. Both men probably knew better than to refuse. Besides, the pie looked and smelled delicious, and they surely wouldn't want to be rude. "It's on the kitchen table in there. I'll get it for you. Eat your pie and drink your coffee. I'll be right back." She set the tray and third mug on the coffee table.

Stryker did not normally eat sweets; however, the pie was well made. The crust was firm yet moist, and the apples had been pre-cooked prior to being baked. Mrs. Rooney used plenty of sugar, and she'd added cinnamon to the filling. He and Stoney finished the pie before she came back.

A moment later, Mrs. Rooney returned from the kitchen carrying the painting. The two men jumped to their feet. "Here you are, Mister Stryker. Alex wanted to build a house like it for me. I don't like it. Don't like the color. Don't like the shape. Take it, please." She handed the painting to Stryker. It was a little over twelve inches high and around eighteen inches wide fully framed. Sure enough, it pictured a yellow house. "Next house I want will have to be a single story. We're getting old. We don't need to be traipsing up and down stairs in old age. Take it before the damn fool comes back and changes his mind."

Stryker took the painting and studied it for a moment. Although the mixed breed had a good education, he was still at a loss to know what constituted good art. The painting offered him no clue either. "Thank you, Mrs. Rooney." He set the painting on the chair behind him and pulled the wad of money from his pocket. After counting out eight of the twenties, he gave them to Mrs. Rooney.

"That's too much," she said, taking the money.

"Keep it," Stryker replied, as he bent to pick up the painting. "I would appreciate it if you had something to wrap around it."

"Oh! I think we may yet have the wooden case Alex brought it home in. It's by the rear fireplace. I hope he hasn't used it for kindling!" Mrs. Rooney scurried back into the kitchen.

She dashed away so quickly; you'd think he was back there preparing to burn the case. Stryker followed her. They met in the doorway with Mrs. Rooney clutching the two-foot by-two-foot balsa-wood case.

"It wasn't burned!" Mrs. Rooney thrust the casing out to Stryker.

Stryker took it, dropped to one knee, and slipped the painting in the case. He stood up, placed it under his arm, and headed back into the living room to get his hat.

"I'll be on my way, Mrs. Rooney. Thanks for the coffee and pie."

"Emeline."

Stryker grabbed the Stetson off the chairback and turned around. "What's that, ma'am?"

"Emeline," Mrs. Rooney repeated from the kitchen doorway. "That's my given name. If you're ever back this way, you may call me Emeline."

"Will do," Stryker said and slapped on his hat. He spun on his heel and left out the front door. A few seconds later, Stoney stepped through the door as well and mounted the bay. Using the saddle rope, Stryker fastened the case on the saddle horn. Stoney waited for him to finish and climb on the roan, and they rode off.

When they got back to the herd, Stoney broke off and joined up with Alex Rooney. Stryker kept riding, skirted a wide detour around the cattle, and brought the roan onto the road to Denver. About a mile further, he rode past four cowboys bringing the forty head of cattle back to the main herd. They eyed him somewhere between *thanks* and suspicion.

Night had fallen in Denver when Stryker rode into town. He crossed the bridge over Cherry Creek and entered the west end of Larimar Street. Lanterns were lit along both sides of the street. He rode past Seventeenth Street where he saw and heard the Tivoli Club a few doors down. Although dark, it was too early for liquor to have heavily soaked the gambler's brains. It would get a lot louder in another hour or two. After coming to Eighteenth and Larimar, he stabled the roan and untied the painting to carry into the Windsor. Wilson, the uniformed attaché who'd served him and Mrs. Mackey two days earlier in the library, walked by with a tray loaded with a champagne bottle and four glasses. Stryker grabbed him by the arm, swinging the man around to a full stop. If Wilson hadn't been an expert carrying trays, he would have dropped his. "Go tell Mrs. Mackey I want to see her."

"Uh, can I drop off these drinks?" Wilson asked.

Stryker tightened his grip. "That can wait."

Wilson stepped to the library and set the tray on a reading table. He rushed to the staircase and disappeared up the stairs. Sixty seconds later, he bounded down the steps.

"She said for you to come to her room, room *440*, sir." Wilson bowed and walked smartly to the library and picked up the drink tray.

Stryker thought it odd the woman would invite him to her room, but he made for the stairs. Upon reaching the fourth floor, he headed down the hall, passing an elderly couple in formal attire. He rapped on the door numbered *440*. A woman, not Mrs. Mackey, cracked open the door.

"She'll see you in a moment, sir," the plump, rosy-faced, wardrobe maid cheerfully said. She opened the door wider, and Stryker entered the room. He stood in its center and surveyed the room decorated with vintage French furniture, a pink chandelier, pink lamps with frilly shades, a white six-foot high armoire, and a fireplace framed with a pink surround. The many shades of pink and white throughout the sitting room assaulted his eyes. Walls, carpet, lamps, and stuffed chairs were a one-room tsunami of the two colors. Stryker then realized Mrs. Mackey rented two rooms, one as the sitting room where he stood, and a second was used as her bedroom.

The wardrobe assistant disappeared into the bedroom and closed the door. Stryker could hear them talking with hurried voices on the other side of the door. A properly dressed woman in the 1880s needed help getting dressed. Wearing bustles, corsets, and whatever other contraptions women tortured themselves with, they *couldn't* dress themselves. Putting the stuff on and taking it off was such a tremendous struggle, Stryker marveled that the human race was able to survive. *Honey, after getting undressed, I'm too tired to fuck.* A wardrobe maid is not to be confused with a handmaiden. A handmaiden usually wore a long red gown to signify she was fertile and could conceive a child. The color red meant she still had menstrual cycles. Wealthy men in those days were often married to older women who could not have children (or couldn't get their clothes off*),* and if he wanted a child to carry on with his estate, well, the handmaiden helped him out. Probably didn't hurt if she were fetching as well. Little surprise then, that wives looked upon handmaidens with contempt. A few minutes later, Mrs. Mackey threw open the door. She emerged with her wardrobe maid in tow. Marie wore a pink silk robe with white rabbit fur puffed around the collar, wrists, and front edges. The gown reached to the floor to hide her silk slippers. She had yet to get properly dressed for dinner.

"Stryker! You have the painting?" Marie exclaimed, wearing a broad smile that showed all her teeth. Her eyes glowed with excitement as she stared at the case, and not at Stryker.

Stryker held it out to her.

"Help me take it out, Helen," Marie said. The wardrobe maid took the case. She attempted to withdraw the painting while holding the case under her arm, but she compressed the flimsy wood so tightly, she couldn't pull it out.

Stryker stepped up to help her. "I'll hold the case. You pull it out." Together, Helen and Stryker got the painting out.

"Oh, it's so beaut…" The smile fell from Marie's face. "That's not the painting."

"Shit," Stryker cursed.

"It's not the same house. It's yellow but not the right one, and the painting is too small. The one I bought was bigger, more like two feet by four feet."

"Where's Sophia?" Stryker growled.

"She's gone," Marie said.

"Where?"

"I don't know, Stryker. Have you heard, Helen?"

"No ma'am."

"Stryker, it may not mean anything, but the night Sophia disappeared, Oliver did too. And one more thing, a cook was found stabbed to death in the kitchen."

Stryker spun on his heels and marched from the room made more repulsive by what he'd just learned. He slammed the door behind him.

Downstairs, Stryker walked up to the front desk and shoved a young couple aside. The mixed breed was not in a good mood. Those who crossed him, and threatened his life, usually paid with their own, but nothing raised his ire more than being made a fool. The husband started to protest but thought better of it. Werner, standing behind the desk waved his hand at them as if to say, "Don't."

"C'mon," the husband whispered to his wife, and they quickly adjourned to the reading room across the lobby. Once there, the husband peeked out to see what the ill-mannered man at the counter would do next.

"Where's Sophia?" Stryker demanded

"She left," Werner replied curtly, smug satisfaction written on his face. He noticed Stryker's menacing countenance and added, "I mean she quit, sir. She and Oliver quit together."

Stryker reached across the counter and grabbed the front of Werner's jacket. "Where? Dammit!"

"I heard 'em say somethin' about a train," Werner offered. He tried to shrink down as if preparing to duck under the counter. However, the train information was enough for Stryker to release him and leave the hotel.

Stryker went immediately to the station, and when he found out where Sophia and Oliver had gone, he bought tickets for the newly completed Missouri Pacific which ran from Denver to Saint Louis. He didn't bring the roan.

CHAPTER NINE

I t took three days. He slept on the train. Got off only to eat and use the toilet. His mood never brightened. No reading newspapers, books, or other reading material; Stryker just sat and brooded. Passengers sensed Stryker's frame of mind and left him alone. No one sat next to him, or across from him at his customary seat rear of the car. One man stood for sixty miles to keep from seating close to him. A dark, foreboding cloud surrounded the man and violence only needed a small spark. Fortunately for those on the train, it never lit.

Stryker stepped off the train in Saint Louis at two 'clock in the afternoon. Named after the French King, Louis IX, the city had a population of around four hundred thousand. He realized he had only a slight chance of finding Sophia and Oliver, even if they had remained in the midwestern town. The pair would probably need to pawn at least some of the jewelry and artwork and convert it into cash, money for living expenses, or traveling. He sought out a pawn shop and found one on Olive Street. In fact, he found three. Two on the North side of the street a block apart and one two blocks down. None of the shops looked upscale to handle expensive jewelry like Mrs. Mackey would have owned. He walked into the first shop he came to, anyway. The wooden sign nailed above the door read "Rod's Pawn" in black letters on a crude one-by-two-foot white board.

Inside the small shop, wooden shelving lined both side walls, and the rear wall as well. Used clothing lay in numbered bins on the shelving. Didn't smell all that good either. A counter sat in the middle of the floor. A cash box was on top of the counter. A short man, maybe two inches over five feet tall, stood behind it. He was alone in the shop.

"You have jewelry or art in any of these pawn shops?" Stryker asked, standing in the doorway. He figured he might inquire about the other two shops as well. He didn't ask if the man were Rod.

"No. Mister, you're in the wrong part of town for that stuff. People come in on Monday, pawn clothes, and come back on Friday when they get paid to pick 'em up. We're low-end here."

"Where's a shop that'll pawn expensive stuff? Jewelry, guns, and art." Stryker threw in guns too, a common pawn item that could fetch high dollars.

"Go to the west edge of town. That's where the rich live in St. Louis. There's a shop there. Not called a pawn-shop, though. The wealthy don't like to frequent pawn shops. Too embarrassed. It's called Nikki's Collectibles."

"Trolley or cab."

"Catch the trolley on Market, three streets that way." Rod, or whatever his name was, hooked a thumb over his right shoulder and went back to counting inventory.

Stryker backed out of the shop, walked to the street corner, and turned right. He crossed Pine and Chestnut Streets to the broad thoroughfare of Market Street. Horse trolleys ran busily on the street, heading east and west. He hopped on one headed west and dropped a nickel, the required fare, into the Johnson Farebox. Before too long, spaces between the buildings widened and the structures, some business some residential, took on a cleaner, more upscale appearance. He spied a clean white single-story building on the north side of the street with green trim along the corners and the two front windows. A small sign over the matching green door read "Nikki's Collectibles" in gold script lettering. Beneath that was stamped "Hours 9 AM to 9 PM" in white. He stepped off the trolley and walked up to the door.

He turned the brass handle and entered. The interior, stylishly decorated, looked cozy and quaint. Plush forest green carpeting covered the floor, allowing customers to amble about quietly in the room. Stryker counted seven customers, two female couples and three women by themselves. The couples stopped by various items and talked in hushed tones. There were separate sections for different types of *collectibles*. Watches displayed in velvet boxes on round table stands covered with lace doilies stood in one corner. Women's belts, scarves, and hats were on a dark walnut chest along one wall. Open drawers held colorful silk scarves. Belts and hats rested on layered shelving on top. Men's accessories were similarly displayed on a matching chest next to that. Along the opposite wall, female mannequins wore stylish gowns and dresses. Farther along that wall, men's suits hung on the male figures. Jewelry, obviously very expensive, was exhibited in a locked glass case in the rear near a desk holding the cash drawer. Each item had either a red tag, or a green tag, indicating merchandise being held, or for sale. Stryker figured green was for immediate sale. Windows on both sides of the shop provided light, but curiously to him, there were lighted glass lamps with shell shades. Five of them were throughout the interior, and they sat on five-foot pedestals. The lamps had cords connected to them. The lamps provided soft ambient lighting. He might ask about those lights later, he thought. An open archway behind the cash stand led to a room with gun racks.

There was one additional accouterment. One not for sale. A tall man stood between the cash counter and the firearms door, and he held a Greener twelve-gauge shotgun resting in the crook of an elbow. The gun was not for sale either. The broad-shouldered, serious-looking fellow, appeared ready to use it if called upon. But the customers milled about shopping and ignored him.

Two more women stood by the cash drawer. One held what appeared to be a ledger and a pencil, and they were apparently discussing something in the ledger. Maybe one of them was the owner. Stryker walked to the counter.

"May I help you?" The woman with the ledger and pencil looked up and asked. She was short, but reasonably thin, and appeared to be in her mid-thirties. Her smile was wide and friendly. The reading glasses resting down her nose made her seem business-like, yet more appealing. Shoulder-length raven hair parted on one side, she wore a green silk blouse and a pair of tan slacks. She did a good job filling out the front of the blouse. The woman beside her looked several years older, a half head taller, and filled out her clothing all over. The face wasn't bad. But that woman carried thirty pounds too many.

"You have any art?" Stryker asked.

"We do have a few pieces," the shorter woman replied. "They're in that rack over there." She pointed the pencil toward the wooden tiered display rack in a corner.

Stryker saw the rack she meant and strode over to it. The shotgun toter followed him with his eyes. Eight paintings hung on the rack. There were four tiered rows, two to a row, making the two front paintings easily seen, and the tops of the rest in ascending order. A quick search told him none were of a yellow house. He returned to the counter.

"Looking for a particular piece. A yellow house."

"Nothing like that now. Why so choosey?" The woman with the ledger asked. She acted as if she could be the owner. She pressed the ledger against her chest, putting that aside for a moment. "Sorry, My name's Nikki. I own the place," she said, releasing a hand from the ledger. She held it out to Stryker. "And this is Helen," Nikki said, pointing at the woman beside her. Helen did not offer her hand. "Max is my guard," Nikki added.

"Stryker," he replied, taking her hand. Nikki had a firm grip, and he liked that. "The painting was stolen. I'm attempting to retrieve it for a client. Jewelry was taken also. Any jewelry come in the last couple of days?"

"Stryker," Nikki repeated, giving him a long study. "We try very hard not to take in stolen merchandise. I want you to know that."

"All right."

"We did get a necklace in yesterday. I think it was expensive. It's being appraised." Nikki glanced at her assistant, who nodded in return.

"Describe it."

"Gold chain. Diamonds hang at the bottom and are shaped with the initials, MM. The letters are entwined together," Nikki said. "I don't ask for names. We're very discreet here. We only use receipt tokens, but I would like to know… does the owner live in St. Louis?"

"No."

"Stryker," Nikki hesitated. She locked on his pale gray eyes. "Can you give me a reason why I should trust you?"

"I'll buy the painting. Not here to steal."

"I don't want violence in here between you and whoever stole the painting, or the jewelry."

"I'm sure they don't either," Stryker allowed.

"Why don't you go to the police?"

"My client doesn't want publicity."

Nikki acknowledged that with an uneasy smile.

"Who brought it in? When will they return?"

"They. You keep saying 'they,' but yes, there was a young man and a woman. They said they'd be back the day after tomorrow. Don't know the time."

Stryker raised a forefinger to the Stetson. "Thanks." Then he swung about and walked from the store.

"I don't like him, Miss," The shotgun guard said, stepping up to the counter. He'd kept his eyes on the mixed breed the entire time he was in the shop. "He's a violent man. I know the type. And what he said about stuff being stolen could be a load of crap. Maybe we should go to the police ourselves."

"I think not," Nikki said. "Our customers wouldn't be comfortable with police in here. They're nervous enough. Most of 'em come in the back door as it is. You'll just have to handle everything, Max."

"No sweat," Max said, patting the shotgun.

Stryker used the extra day to find a telegraph office and send a report to Senator Hearst. He only told the senator he had a promising lead in St. Louis. The rest of the time he stayed close to the shop. Not so close to where he'd be noticed, but close enough to watch for the couple in case they returned early. They never showed, and he wondered if they'd show on the second day. Then he had irritating doubts they would. *Shit.* He figured they would use the front door; however, he did scout out the back as well. During the time he surveyed that entrance, he saw several people, usually by themselves, come and go. There were two couples, both women, who used the rear door.

Across the street, he located a cafe with a window facing the front where he could watch Nikki's shop. It wasn't directly across the street. It was two buildings down, but he still had a good view of the front door. Clouds rolled in by late afternoon and a light drizzle began to fall. The horse trolley ran every half hour. Stryker saw no one get on or off though. Farther west on the street, the homes got larger and more widely spaced. Mansions like the Mallinckrodt (of Mallinckrodt Chemicals) stately house on Vandeventer Place were lavish displays of accumulated wealth; it was a three-story home with a stone foundation, masonry front, and a steep, gabled roof. Soon, brewers like Lemp and Anheuser-Busch would erect even more magnificent and extravagant mansions. Stryker wasn't interested in house shopping though. He was here to get the painting, and he was in a particularly bad mood.

Sophia and Oliver didn't appear that day. Stryker took the trolley back to the middle of town and got a room at a two-story boarding house. He had steak, potatoes, biscuits, and coffee for dinner prepared by a woman named Mrs. Clevenger. Mrs. Clevenger was a widowed schoolteacher who taught high school English. She was not bad looking and she paid extra attention to his wants. "Is there anything I can do for you, Mister Stryker? Anything at all?" Too bad Stryker wasn't interested in added *services*. He picked up a copy of the *St. Louis Republic* and retired to his room to read the newspaper. Lying in bed in just his short-legged underwear, he positioned the lantern on its nightstand so he could have better light, and he read several articles, including a lengthy one on President Grover Cleveland. Then he turned down the lantern. Lying there awake for the better part of an hour, he was thinking about the three southern rustlers and how he probably didn't need to kill them. Then, he finally drifted off to sleep.

Stryker woke before the sun came up. He cleaned himself using the wash bowl on the chest of drawers, shaved in its mirror, and completed his toiletries before going downstairs for breakfast. Mrs. Clevenger had griddled French toast and ham for him. He sat at the breakfast table alone. Evidently, she'd heard him stirring upstairs and got up early to cook the morning meal. It wasn't his usual breakfast fare. He'd had steak last night anyway. She'd doused the egg-battered bread with lots of butter and powdered sugar. He cleaned his plate.

"Will you be staying another night?" she'd asked. When he told her he didn't think so, she said, "I hope you'll come back this way some-time." *Women are hard to figure out*, Stryker thought. A lot of them were put off by his fearsome appearance and still, others didn't seem to be bothered by how he looked. Regardless, he wasn't about to change. He couldn't change.

Stryker hailed a horse-drawn cab and arrived back at Nikki's Collectibles an hour before the shop opened. It was a clear day, the clouds from the prior day dissipated, and the sun had begun to warm the morning. After strolling around Nikki's and the buildings adjacent to it, Wong's Laundry and Ernie's Barbershop, he walked to the restaurant and ordered a cup of coffee to watch and wait.

A buggy cab pulled in front of the pawn shop fifteen minutes ahead of opening time. No one got out.

At nine o'clock someone–Stryker wasn't able to tell if it were Nikki or Helen–opened the front door and switched the "CLOSED" sign to "OPEN."

Sophia and Oliver stepped out of the cab. Although partially blocked by the rig, Stryker could see that Oliver carried a rolled-up painting under his arm. The two of them entered Nikki's.

Stryker sat the cup on the table with a thud, spilling some of the coffee he hadn't finished. He stepped from the café and walked briskly up the street past the cab where the driver sat, and cracked open the door to the pawn shop. Sophia and Oliver stood at the counter with their backs to him. Oliver was not exactly next to Sophia, but a step back from her. He was letting Sophia do the talking. The painting lay spread out on the counter, held down with women's brooch pins on the corners. Stryker slipped inside and quietly shut the door.

Max stood at his customary position by the weapons room. He wasn't watching the four people at the counter. Max was eying Stryker, and he had the shotgun pointed at him.

Stryker slipped the razor from his rear pocket, keeping it hidden behind his hip.

"This is the rest of the jewelry I got from my grandmother," Sophia said to Nikki. "It's all of it." She placed the jewelry pieces next to the painting. "And I also brought this painting. It's from Europe from a very famous artist."

"Who's the artist?" Nikki asked. She had seen Stryker come into the shop but said nothing. Helen, helping Sophia with the jewels and painting hadn't noticed him.

"It's signed by him there at the bottom left corner." Sophia pointed at the signature, "Vincent."

"We'll have to appraise all this, you know," Nikki said.

"How much for the first piece?" Sophia asked. She sounded frustrated. Oliver stood close by not saying anything. The piece was a three-carat diamond ringed by blue sapphires.

"We can give you eight-hundred dollars if it appraises out." Nikki glanced nervously at Stryker who'd crept up behind Oliver.

"Like I told you, my grandmother gave me this stuff, so I guess I'll take what you offer. No one should be allowed to have as much money as she had anyway. It's not fair," Sophia spoke as if she'd heard that kind of rhetoric before. "Why didn't she give me cash," Sophia groused.

Max shifted the shotgun away from Stryker. He was too close to Oliver now. The guard was just about to say something when Stryker reached around Oliver–and slit his throat. Oliver dropped to the floor with a whimper.

Stryker leaped behind Sophia and placed the bloody razor on her neck before Oliver hit the floor.

Helen screamed.

Sophia stifled one.

Nikki glared at Stryker.

"Move away from her!" Max yelled, motioning the shotgun from left to right.

"Drop the shotgun," Stryker ordered. "Do it now, or I'll kill her."

Stryker dug in the blade's tip beneath her left ear, drawing blood.

"Drop it, Max," Nikki said, still glaring at Stryker.

Max had enough sense to stoop down and set the gun on the floor instead of dropping it.

"Now, kick it over here," Stryker ordered.

Max nudged the shotgun across the floor with his boot. It wouldn't slide easily on the carpet, and he had to keep pushing it with his foot until he got it next to Stryker.

"Now back away," Stryker ordered.

Max backed up to the weapons door. "If you harm these girls, I'll hunt you down and kill you, mister."

Stryker drew the razor across Sophia's throat. She fell gagging to the carpet and Stryker bent to pick up the shotgun. He wiped the blade on Sophia's sleeve before he stood. Oliver was dead. Sophia would soon be.

"Roll up the painting, Nikki," Stryker said, slipping the razor into his rear pocket. "Keep the jewels."

Stryker kept the Greener pointed at Max as he stepped to the door. Outside, he got in the buggy. "Take me to the train station. The other two don't need you." Stryker handed the driver a twenty-dollar note; the driver snapped the reins.

Stryker didn't know for sure if Oliver or Sophia killed the cook at the Windsor Hotel. It didn't matter to him. However, Oliver had indeed murdered the cook, at Sophia's urging. The cook saw them stealing food in the kitchen and had also seen the jewelry and painting. He had to die.

As often mentioned before, Stryker is the wrong man to cross. However, if someone does, and then dies by his hand, is it murder or suicide?

CHAPTER TEN

"We need the police," Nikki said, her eyes fixed on the bloodied bodies lying in front of the counter.

"Well… what for?" Helen asked, staring at the bodies too.

Nikki tore her eyes away from the gruesome scene and turned to her assistant. "What for? We just had two murders! That's what for."

"We had two thieves executed for stealing, what… thousands of dollars of jewelry. We don't know them. They're not from around here. And we don't even know who owned the jewelry," Helen pointed out.

"How much is that stuff worth?" Max asked, pointing at the jewelry pieces on the counter.

"You offered eight hundred, for the one piece, Nikki. So, what would you sell it for?" Helen asked, with raised eyebrows and a smirky smile.

"Fifteen hundred, maybe two thousand… I guess." Nikki deadpanned. She was staring at the jewelry now.

"And the rest?"

"I'll take these two out and bury 'em," Max quickly offered. "You girls get busy cleaning the carpet."

"I guess we should close the shop for a bit, at least 'til we can clean up the mess," Nikki supplied. She turned back and stared at the bodies. "Can evil do good?"

"Another thing, Nikki," Max said. "That man gave the jewelry to you. If he came back to get them and found out you'd turned them jewels over to the police, he might'n not like it."

"No, he might'n not," Helen said, echoing Max. Her hand streaked to her throat.

"Put the sign on the door, Helen. Get me some towels, Nikki," Max said, kneeling beside Oliver's body. "Hurry, girls. We don't have all day."

Forty-five minutes after leaving Nikki's Collectibles, Stryker was on the Missouri-Pacific headed back to Denver in a decidedly better mood. Taking his accustomed place in the coach, rear seat, back to the wall, he picked up a discarded copy of the *Republic*. *Good*, he thought, it gave him something to read. He kept the rolled-up painting next to him while he read the paper. The sun shone brightly on the Missouri fields and the train was making good time on level ground. He also sat alone. Stryker had grown accustomed to passengers not wanting to sit near him. He knew it wasn't because he was odorous. He released a low grunt at the prospect. He didn't mind, though. He preferred to be alone on the train. Some time afterward, when his ticket was punched by the uniformed conductor, another man, a young man in his mid-twenties worked his way along the aisle and took a seat across from Stryker.

The man wore a dark blue suit with a starched upturned collar. No hat. One couldn't say he was nattily dressed; however, he was not overweight and was in good form. Well-collected, he appeared neat with an air of self-discipline. A glance by Stryker suggested to him the fellow might be in the teaching profession. He looked studious enough with a tattered briefcase and intensely blue eyes, stern enough to be that of a headmaster. He sat quietly, penning something on a tablet.

Stryker read his paper. And that went on for the better part of an hour.

Finally, Stryker laid the newspaper aside and watched the landscape slip past his window.

The teacher-type drew a deep breath as if he'd just finished writing something of weighty importance. Perhaps he had. Regardless, he studied Stryker seated across from him, apparently trying to decide whether or not to initiate a conversation with the menacing-looking man.

"Are you traveling all the way to Denver, sir?" The fellow asked with a friendly smile.

Stryker turned from the window. "That's right."

"I see you have some kind of a drawing rolled up beside you. A small portion inside the roll showed color. Mind if I ask what it is?" The friendly grin remained alight.

Stryker still in a good mood, answered, "It's a painting." He didn't respond with a smile of his own. He wasn't in that good of a mood.

"May I see it?"

"Why?" Stryker's countenance turned threatening.

"I'm sorry," the man apologized. "I'm James. I'm a minister from New York City, Riverside Baptist Church."

"Not interested in salvation, preacher." In the past, other men of the cloth had tried and failed. Stryker had no patience with them, but he hadn't killed any. Yet.

"I have an interest in religious art, nothing more."

"Not religious."

"Okay then. Sorry to bother you." The grin fell away and James went back to his writings.

"And you, what's your scribbling?" Stryker growled, jabbing the return more out of annoyed spitefulness rather than curiosity.

James looked up with a somewhat sheepish grin. "Oh, it's just something I thought about. Might use it in a sermon sometime."

"Read it to me," Stryker demanded. Couldn't say he was being unusually nasty if he was just being himself.

"Well, all right." You could tell James wrestled with not reading it. He wisely chose not to antagonize Stryker with a refusal.

"Here is a man who was born in an obscure village, the

child of a peasant woman. He grew up in another village. He worked in a carpenter shop until He was thirty. Then for three years, He was an itinerant preacher.

He never owned a home. He never wrote a book. He never held an office. He never had a family. He never went to college. He never put His foot inside a big city. He never traveled more than two-hundred miles from where He was born. He never did one of those things which accompany greatness. He had no credentials but Himself...

While still a young man, the tide of popular opinion turned against Him. His friends turned away. One denied Him. He was turned over to His enemies. He went through the mockery of a trial. He was nailed to a cross between two thieves. While he was dying, His executioners gambled for the only piece of property He had on earth–His coat. When He was dead, He was laid in a borrowed grave through the pity of a friend.

Nineteen long centuries have come and gone, and today, He is the centerpiece of the human race and the leader of the column of progress.

I am far within the mark when I say that all the armies that ever marched, all the navies that were ever built, all the parliaments that ever sat, and all the kings who ever reigned put together, have not affected the life of man upon this earth as powerfully as has that one solitary life."

James continued looking at what he'd just read out loud. "I guess there's a few grammatical errors I need to fix."

"It's fine like it is, James."

James Allan Francis (1864-1928) went on to use this essay in a sermon he gave on July 11, 1926. He moved to Los Angeles in 1914 and died there in 1928.

Stryker and James spoke on and off until Kansas City. It was a twelve-hour train ride; however, the trip passed quickly because their conversation filled the time. James did not try to convert Stryker and the mixed breed recounted a few things about himself leaving out much of the violence. When James asked if he'd ever been married, Stryker told him about Leigh at length. Stryker learned James was from Canada and he'd begun preaching when he was twenty-one. Other times the topic drifted into history, Canadian and American, and the two men gleaned historical anecdotes from one another. Overall, Stryker enjoyed the man's company. James left the train in Kansas City to speak at a Baptist tent revival, and Stryker never saw or heard from him again.

Riding the train on to Denver provided no respite from the monotonous wheel clacking, even with someone Stryker disliked. It took two days. He read collections of writings by Thomas Paine; *Common Sense, Rights of Man,* and *Age of Reason* he'd picked up in a bookstore in Kansas City to fill time during the day. He tried to sleep during the one night on the trip, but most of the time he just dozed on and off.

Stryker did have a moment of self-recrimination during the night, perhaps brought on by his meeting with the Baptist pastor. Killing Sophia and Oliver wasn't entirely necessary. Oliver may not have been part of the original theft–although he eventually was. Sophia was a woman, and the two of them weren't armed. But then again, he thought, those three southern rustlers and the husband and wife in Denver might still be alive if not for Sophia's lies. Stryker dozed.

Would the pale-eyed killer still have taken Sophia's life if the five aforementioned lives had been spared? It's a hard guess. At times Stryker struggled with himself over such decisions, especially since his close call in Tahoe where he almost died and was nursed back to health by a good Samaritan female doctor. For a while after that, he tried to make a change. And now, just recently, the Baptist Pastor had made an influence. But he had too many hardened scars for it to be easy. One thing that had changed in him was he was able to find some good in other people. Probably not so much in himself, though. His life–well, it was still governed by his own strict moral code, and he remained a dangerous man to cross.

He kept the rolled painting by his side the entire train ride.

Stryker arrived back in Denver at four in the afternoon and straight away marched to the Windsor Hotel to find Marie. They met in the lobby reading room.

"Yes, that's it," Mrs. Mackey sounding relieved. "Where did you find it?"

"St. Louis," Stryker replied.

"My goodness! Sophia?"

"Yes."

"I thought she was trustworthy. I never suspected she would have taken a nickel from me. Guess I'm not as good a judge of character as I thought," Mrs. Mackey said, plumping her rear down in a stuffed chair. She looked up at Stryker. "What should we do with the painting?"

"I'm taking it to your husband," Stryker replied, rolling up the painting.

"Well, thank you for getting it back," she said. "Hope it wasn't a lot of trouble?" She added, with the question written on her face.

"Not too much."

"Good, thank you again." Mrs. Mackey smiled with relief.

"So long, Marie." Stryker turned and walked from the reading room.

Stryker left the hotel and headed to the train station where he checked on the roan. Then he bought tickets to San Francisco.

CHAPTER ELEVEN

Two and a half days later, Stryker arrived in San Francisco at half-past three in the afternoon with the painting and without further mishap. It was a long boring train ride. He didn't mind the boredom, though. Mission accomplished.

He stabled the roan in one of the Ferry House boarding stalls and took the Market Street cable car to the Palace Hotel. As a welcome home to him, the skies in the city were clear. Every time Stryker revisited after being away, it seemed as if the city had grown. New buildings and new businesses had sprouted. Maybe he hadn't noticed it the last time he was here because of the rain, but he could see it now. As he sat in the car, he briefly speculated where it was all headed. Commerce growth on every street. Banks, showcased in ever-towering brick and stone buildings, brokerages for investment and speculation competed with them. Stores with glass windows displayed the latest fashions. He couldn't help the feeling that men like him were being passed by, shoved aside actually. Ruefully, he had to admit, it was probably a good thing.

The Palace Hotel never failed to impress him. The Grand Court, an elegant carriage entrance to parade the rich and famous, greeted him as he stepped inside, and he couldn't help but glance up at the seven stories of white columned balconies. Too bad William Ralston couldn't have seen it finished. Driven to financial ruin, he drowned himself two months before his fabulous dream hotel opened. Men often dream and exhaust themselves laboring on enormous projects, often never seeing the fruits of their labor. Others enjoy the grandeur while the men who created the grandness lay in their graves. Stryker entered the lobby and crossed over the marble floor to the massive front desk, a dark rich enormous mahogany counter.

"You're here for the senator, Mister Stryker?" The desk clerk with the nameplate on his uniform jacket that said "Steven" recognized him, and knew Hearst always wanted to see him right away. He never knew why, and he never asked.

"Yes."

"Sir, Steven at the front desk," the clerk announced into the speaking tube. "The senator wishes to see you now, Mister Stryker." He nodded with a stiff smile. "Go right up, sir." Then he immediately called after Stryker. "Sir, room *722* is yours."

Stryker worked his way through two crowded groups of conferees wearing conference badges to the rising room, garnering curious stares along the way. He ignored them. He was used to it, but he sensed his time and place *were* being passed by. Five men crowded in with him. "Seventh floor," he growled to the operator. They must have wondered what a rough 'cut' like him was going to do on the top, most expensive, floor. They got off on the third floor.

A hotel attaché opened the door to the senator's suite. "Good to see you again, sir." He was also used to Stryker's preferential treatment by Hearst. "Please come in."

The same plush green carpet, rich dark wood furniture, and expansive view out the window greeted Stryker. Cigar smoke hung in the air. At least Hearst and his hotel room hadn't changed. Stryker entered and swept the Stetson from his head. He tossed it on the conference table.

"Stryker." George Hearst never raised his voice, but he was relieved to see the mixed breed. After all, he'd recommended the man. Upon seeing the rolled painting under Stryker's arm, he said, "Heard you got it."

"Yes." Stryker brushed his hat aside and unrolled the painting on the table.

"Don't look like much, does it?" Hearst said.

"No."

"Reece," Hearst called to the attaché standing by the door. "Send for Mister Mackey. Tell him we have what he's been waiting for." He turned back to Stryker. "Shouldn't be long. I believe he's here in San Francisco. Marie sent a telegraph to tell us you had the painting, so he didn't go back to Virginia City." Hearst clinked the glass pouring cognac into a crystal snifter. "You, Stryker?" Hearst held the bottle ready to pour another.

"I need a bath." Stryker ran a hand through his hair.

"He'll want to thank you, pay you," Hearst said. He lifted his glass in a salute to Stryker.

Stryker left Hearst with the painting. He strode down the hall to room *722*. His room was only a bedroom with a bathroom, not like the senator's two-suite penthouse, but it looked damn good to him, and it didn't take much time to draw a bath, shed his clothing, and settle into the hot soapy water. *Job done*. Yeah, a few setbacks, but not too many. He closed his eyes and rested the back of his head on the rear of the tub, and took a long breath. He'd almost dozed off when he heard the door latch open.

"Thought it might take at least ten minutes to get settled in the tub, and you might want a beer," Morgan called, walking across the carpeted floor to the bathroom. She appeared in the doorway holding a frosted mug of beer.

Stryker didn't know which looked better, the beer or Morgan. *Okay, Morgan did, but the mug was a nice accouterment*. She wore a brown tweed sport jacket, cream-colored silk blouse, and gray wool skirt. Her brunette hair was parted on one side and swept behind an ear. The woman looked damn fine.

"After business is concluded with George and John, let's go to the Cliff House for dinner," Morgan said, handing the beer to Stryker.

Stryker sat up in the tub. She looked too well dressed to take off her clothes now, besides he didn't know how much time he had before meeting with Hearst and Mackey. He sipped the brew and watched

Morgan bring the bathroom stool around to sit. She propped a foot on the cross strut and leaned back against the wall. He liked the way she could strike a casual, yet elegant pose. She relaxed naturally, confident within herself. *Quite a woman, that Morgan.*

"Have much trouble?" Morgan asked.

"Some." Stryker took another sip. "Got delayed a little."

"Well, you finish your bath." Morgan got to her feet. "Come get me when you're through with the men. I'll be in the lobby. There's a carriage waiting in the entrant court, and we have an open table at the Cliff. We can talk about the painting over dinner if you like." She stopped at the doorway. "Okay with you, Stryker?"

Stryker lifted the beer mug a few inches higher as an answer. Morgan smiled in return and disappeared from the doorway. A moment later, he heard the room door open and then close. Resting his arm with the mug on the edge of the tub, he settled back in the soap suds. He finished the beer before all the frost wore off the glass. Hearst had asked Morgan what she saw in him. He even wondered that himself.

He'd gotten out of the tub, dried off, and been lying on the bed in a bathrobe for an hour when someone rapped on the door. Rising to answer, but before he opened the door, he noticed a note slipped underneath. He stooped to pick up the folded card. It read, *"Senator Hearst is waiting for you."*

"Come in, Stryker," Hearst bellowed when the young attaché swung open the door to the senator's room. John Mackay was seated by the conference table. It appeared he and Hearst had sat there for a while; their cognac glasses were almost empty. Hearst stood. Mackay folded a few papers and stuffed them in his coat pocket. Maybe, Stryker figured, they'd been discussing matters other than the painting spread on the table. John stood and extended his hand to Stryker. They shook hands.

"A drink, Stryker?" Hearst asked. Without waiting for Stryker to answer, he poured cognac into a glass and set it on the table. "Have a seat."

"That's it, huh?" Mackay said, eying the artwork spread out on the table. "Don't look like much, does it." He glanced up to Stryker who'd drawn up a chair to sit. "Have much trouble? I mean, did you have to kill anybody?" Mackay joked.

"I never ask about that, John," Hearst warned. "You don't want to know either."

The smile left Mackay's face. "Really? I wasn't serious. But, you didn't, did you?"

"No," Stryker said, sipping the cognac.

"Good, how about a thousand dollars? That sound 'bout right?" Mackay withdrew his checkbook.

Hearst sensed something more. "All right, but *did* you kill anyone getting the painting?"

"He already answered that," Mackay said, looking first at Hearst and then Stryker.

"Seven."

"Told you not to ask, John," Hearst said.

"How about ten thousand?" Mackay directed the question more to Hearst than Stryker.

"I think that's a more suitable fee, John."

Mackay completed the check and passed it to Stryker.

"University President named Holden. He needs a donation. If he's rid of the socialist demonstrating there, give him some money." Stryker took the check and slipped it into his shirt pocket. He finished the cognac, rose from the table, and walked from the room.

"Good God," Mackay stuttered. "Why didn't he say seven in the first place?"

"You asked how many he *had* to kill."

"Guess I better talk to that man Holden," Mackey said. "And I'll have two men return the painting to France and the van Gogh family. I doubt the damn thing will ever be worth any money," Mackay grumbled. He spun his glass a few times on the table and then lifted it to take the last swallow.

Morgan was sitting in an overstuffed chair opposite the front desk and reading the afternoon *Examiner* when Stryker stepped from the rising room. He saw her before she saw him. He walked up and addressed the opened paper, "Let's go eat."

The newspaper was quickly folded and set aside. Morgan stood and grabbed a wool coat off the back of her chair. Stryker helped her put it on. "Can we go for a walk on the beach after dinner?"

Stryker realized the need for a long coat. "Reckon so."

The two-mile ride up Geary Street to the Cliff House took thirty-four minutes. Although not as hilly as many of the San Francisco thorough-fares, they had to make numerous stops at cross streets along the way. Not much was said between Morgan and Stryker as they rode in the carriage. It was as if neither knew how to broach a topic to close the chasm since their last time together. So, they rode most of the trip in silence. Morgan did point out a new brick building on the corner of Geary and Divisadero Street. Stryker grunted a muted reply. Morgan gave up after that.

First built in 1863, the Cliff House had a glamorous yet troubled past. Fire destroyed it more than once, and it was later permanently closed. In 1887, a dynamite-laden schooner ran aground, exploded, and demolished the north wing. However, during Morgan and Stryker's visit, it had been restored and they had a hard time finding a place to park the carriage among the thousand rigs at the hitching racks.

The place was packed with people enjoying the dining, dancing, and plain ole partying. Fortunately, Morgan's table was still reserved for her. Perhaps because she dropped the senator's name when making the reser-vation. They stepped from the carriage, entered, and wove their way through crowded smoke-filled halls, parlors, and bars with Morgan holding Stryker's hand on the way to the dining room. Loud and boister-ous, the Cliff House was not to Stryker's liking, but Morgan just laughed and pulled him along. He wanted the woman to enjoy herself. Several couples recognized Morgan and entreated her and Stryker to join them. Fortunately for Stryker, and the couples, Morgan didn't linger with them after introductions were made, politely turning down their requests. Stryker began to suspect Morgan wasn't totally wrapped up in her mining activities for Hearst while he was away on missions for the senator. That was okay, he was beginning to enjoy *her* enjoyment. It was one of the few times Stryker loosened up a bit. Still, he had difficulty forming a smile. More than one woman beseeched him to stay and talk. They were curious, most likely. He was the only male not wearing a suit and he kind of stood out in his denim and leather. He didn't own a suit and Morgan never risked buying one he'd never wear. The male counterparts weren't so insistent. Morgan finally got them through the crowds to the reserved table next to a window, overlooking Seal Rocks and the ocean.

Morgan ordered wine, Stryker whiskey. She had lobster. He had steak. Neither opted for dessert, although both had coffee. She had a foamed cream with hers. His was black. She asked him about the painting and he told her how he got it without mentioning the killings.

"Let's go for a walk along the beach," Morgan suddenly announced. She placed her cup on the saucer. Ocean Beach stretched for three miles south of the restaurant. She gazed out the window. "There's a full moon. We can watch the waves roll in."

Stryker figured Morgan wanted fresh air. He did too. "Let's go." He rose and helped her don the wool coat. After another journey amongst the maze of smokey rooms, and politely rejecting requests to join acquaintances, they made it out the front entrance. From there, Stryker led Morgan across the restaurant grounds and down the winding rocky path through lush ice plants to the sandy beach.

They stomped in soft sand toward the water where the sand was firm and walked parallel to the crashing waves, glowing white in the moonlight.

"I hadn't realized they were so loud." Morgan grabbed Stryker's arm with both hands and huddled closer. Stryker swung Morgan around so that he was between her and the surf. He put an arm around her shoulders and pulled her tight against him while they continued walking.

"There's a storm out at sea bringing wind and high surf. Not a good night to go swimming, Morgan." Even she wants to swim in the nude, Stryker mused.

The thunderous waves reminded Stryker of cannon fire, but he kept that to himself. They passed one other couple coming in the opposite direction and exchanged greetings. The wind gusts grew stronger after they'd walked a half mile. It swept Morgan's hair behind her and she bent into the wind. Stryker tugged the Stetson down tighter.

"Let's get out of the wind," Morgan said pointing to a sheltered trough nestled between two dunes covered with ice plants. They trudged through the loose sand to the small dune slack where Stryker sat and pulled Morgan down beside him. They sat for a while, huddled out of the wind, and watched the waves break. A ship with lit lanterns came into view about a mile offshore. Neither spoke until it passed out of sight.

"I miss you when you're gone," Morgan said.

"Think about you, too."

A few more minutes passed and Morgan said, "I want you. Right here, right now." She pushed Stryker on his back. Then she stood, opened her coat, pulled up her skirt, and sat astride Stryker's thighs.

As she unbuckled his belt and worked open the fly buttons, Stryker was hoping Morgan wore undergarments with the appropriate opening. He didn't think she'd planned this, and he figured he'd have to rip them off or punch his manhood through. That would be difficult and maybe painful. Stryker was tough, but not that tough, no matter how hard he got. Not a problem. Morgan wore slitted bloomers. He lifted his hips and she worked his denims down off his hips. There was an opening in his cut-off union suit as well. In a few moments, her angelic hands had him rock hard.

She scooted forward and settled down on him with her legs folded behind and outside Stryker's thighs. Slowly, at first, taking in the fullness of him with measured pleasure. Once he was in as far as she could take, Morgan straightened her arms, leaned forward, and placed her hands on Stryker's shoulders. Then she began to lift and up and down, taking her time with each rise and fall. After each downward move, she stayed a while and wiggled her hips, feeling the tip of him press up against that sensitive area inside.

Stryker placed his hands on Morgan's hips to make sure she didn't raise too far and come down to bend him the wrong way. That happened to him once before and hurt like hell. He knew a girl could get carried away and not realize she could injure a fellow, so he'd help guide her while she enjoyed herself. After several minutes of bumping up and down, Morgan became more active and more forceful, and he tightened his grip on her hips.

For Morgan's part, she was working harder, ratcheting up her pleasure. The waves came from down the beach and rolled toward them to break. It seemed as if the breaking crescendo rolling up the beach was in sync with a building orgasm. This happened several times, but her climax hadn't happened. She worked harder, faster.

Stryker thought maybe Morgan could use a little help and he slipped his fingers down past the clitoral hood to touch her. With her knees spread outside his hips, her clitoris was fully exposed against his fingertips. He began gently teasing down both sides of the swollen nub and made light circles on top. Occasionally, he'd insert a finger inside her for lubrication and moisten her clitoris. Bringing her along with just the right amount of patience, she stayed still and let his fingers work. After a while, he rubbed a little harder, a little faster.

Waves were growing louder now and Morgan was getting closer, matching her sensual pleasure with the sound of pounding waves. A wave rolled up the beach, crashing behind, and she pressed down on the fingers and his rigid penis, holding its head against that special spot, and did a slow grind. Her inner thighs began to spasm and Morgan had a long gut-wrenching climax. A wave of ecstasy washed through her body as another roller broke, and her entire body shook in passionate rapture. Afterward, she fell forward onto Stryker's chest. Then his fingers started on her again. Gradually she felt a growing need and she had another orgasm, along with another crashing wave. Then again. And again. They kept coming. With the waves. Waves broke way down the beach and rolled toward them. Inside Morgan too, building… cresting… breaking. Coming on one after another. Morgan lost count. She was working hard now, her hands dug into his shoulders. His damn fingers were relentless. He'd hold them still, pressing against her engorged clitoris when she came, and then he'd start up again. There was no control; she couldn't stop having them. Why would she want to?

Eventually, Morgan gave out. Her knees started to get sore from rubbing in the sand, and she pulled Stryker's hand away. She was getting a little sensitive. *My God, how many were there?* Somewhere in the high teens was all she could guess. *Can a woman die from too many orgasms?* "Stryker, you need to come. I can't go anymore," she gasped.

He held her hips and began to work on his release, holding Morgan close to his chest as he slowly pumped in and out. He sped up and it didn't take long. Morgan's ardor had aroused him as well. After he came, he waited a bit and then started working on another. Two was enough. It was Morgan's night. He pulled a handkerchief from his pocket and used it when he pulled out after the last one. Damn thoughtful of the mixed breed.

Later, as they climbed the steps to where the carriage waited, Stryker felt Morgan quivering under his arm around her, and he held her tighter thinking she was cold.

Morgan wasn't cold. Her body was still sexually and electrically, charged, and that's why she trembled. Waves in the sea and waves rolling through her body had been euphoric and passionate. She was still swollen, sensitive, and throbbing. Stryker would probably stay with her tonight. Hold her while they slept. They may or may not have sex again. It didn't matter. Just being close was enough. Like always, he would leave before dawn. That would be okay. She wanted private time. Private time alone when she could do things without worrying about being self-conscious. After he left, she *might* lie on her stomach and her hand *might* find its way between her thighs. She *might* be already wet. If not, she *might* lick her fingers, turn over to touch herself, and think about those wonderful pounding waves.

As for Stryker, he returned to Pescadero and wore his Stetson upon a troubled brow.

NOTES

CHAPTER 2

1. You can read that story in Left to Die; Book 1 in the Evil Stryker Series.

CHAPTER 3

1. Her real name may have been Rachel. Gaby or Rachel, the girl may have used a pseudonym, after all, she did work "cleaning" a French whorehouse
2. The painting, *The Yellow House,* probably wasn't worth much in the 1880s, maybe not more than a couple hundred French francs. Van Goh did sell a piece for that amount. *The Yellow House* has remained in the van Gogh family, and it is on permanent loan to the van Gogh Museum in Amsterdam. It would easily fetch more the US$100 million today.
3. The Great San Francisco Earthquake hit in 1906, killing three-thousand people and toppling half of the buildings in the city, including the Palace Hotel.

CHAPTER 5

1. For a more complete description of a Stryker journey over the Sierras in winter, read *The Christmas Slay*.
2. Van Gogh actually sold two or three paintings. The myth nevertheless persists that the artist only sold one.
3. Adventure is recounted in *Trouble in Tahoe*.

ACKNOWLEDGMENTS

Thanks to my dear wife, Pamela Mitchell, and my indispensable editor, Stacey Smekofske.

ABOUT THE AUTHOR

Wes Rand was an Artillery Officer in the U.S. Army during the 1960s. He pays alimony. He doesn't like to golf but lives on a golf course. He has been bucked off a horse and two women.

He has a cabin in the mountains where he writes and hikes while his wife plays golf in Las Vegas. Wes enjoys living under the open skies in Nevada and Utah.

 facebook.com/wes.rand.14

instagram.com/rand.wes